Further praise for *One Life*

'A love letter to an unborn child that cuts to the core of what it means to be a man or a woman in the modern world'　　　　　　　　　　　　　　　TONY PARSONS

'An accomplished and startling debut novel'
Daily Ireland

'The author's own experience of IVF lends authenticity to this charged tale of a career couple whose increasingly desperate attempt to conceive threatens to destroy their relationship'　　　　　　　　　　　　　　　*Grazia*

'Instantly engaging, this is a poignant account of a modern couple – their lives free and career-orientated – and how things change with the question of commitment and children ... The subsequent quest to conceive in the face of infertility is frankly and movingly written'
Big Issue

'For fans of Maggie O'Farrell and Tony Parsons ... this book is a must-read'　　　　　　　　*Birmingham Post*

One Life

REBECCA FRAYN

POCKET
BOOKS

London • New York • Sydney • Toronto

First published in Great Britain by Simon & Schuster UK Ltd, 2006
First published by Pocket Books, 2007
An imprint of Simon & Schuster UK Ltd
A CBS COMPANY

3 5 7 9 10 8 6 4

Simon & Schuster UK Ltd
Africa House
64–78 Kingsway
London WC2B 6AH

www.simonsays.co.uk

Simon & Schuster Australia
Sydney

A CIP catalogue record for this book is
available from the British Library

ISBN-13: 978-1-4165-0270-8
ISBN-10: 1-4165-0270-X

Typeset by Rowland Phototypesetting Ltd,
Bury St Edmunds, Suffolk

Printed and bound in Great Britain by
Cox & Wyman Ltd, Reading Berks

For Finn, Jack and Emmy

The picture was scratched, and the soundtrack intermittently distorting on the bass notes, but all technical shortcomings were overridden by the sheer horror of the image that flickered there. Before us a woman writhed and howled, while between her splayed legs spilled liquid – more liquid than I'd ever imagined the human body could possibly contain. Convulsing and bellowing, she appeared to have no face, her features engulfed by the howling yawn of mouth. Then something crumpled and purple was at last expelled from her, slippery with blood and mucus, its goblin face also contorted by a high-pitched wail, its repellent appearance quite as alarming as the excruciating torments that had produced it.

As the fluorescent lights fizzed and guttered into life again, Mrs Tanner stood with her hand at the switch, surveying the faces of the class, apparently amused at the dazed hush that had fallen across the room.

'Any questions, 3R?' she called cheerily, her voice coming from far away on the winds of whistling faintness. Her mumsy smile seemed sinister now, her very womanliness to embody treachery.

Around me my classmates – thirty teenage girls contemplating their biological destiny. After all those years of shy allusions and giggling playground whispers, this then was what awaited us.

PART ONE

the sea's
the home
from which
i rose
&
homeward
now
the river
goes

Robert Lax

1

We might be children again as we sit here side by side, filled with anxious humility before this stranger, this infertility specialist, as he rests his pious gaze upon us. And now that we're here, if we have to be here – I'm rather hoping he can write us out a prescription which could have it all sorted out without further ado. But it's increasingly apparent from his melancholy patter, that our quest for a child will be an expensive and, quite possibly, a prolonged one. That the treatment will be invasive and the long-term health consequences unknown. That above all, there are no guarantees that we will have anything to show for all our trouble and expense at the end. Somehow the thing I had spent so much of my adult life fearing, has become the very thing I now sought in vain.

In adversity, we quite naturally try to construct a narrative. To trace the underlying cause and effect that brought us to this sad and sorry place. And often I puzzle over how it was that the problems of infertile couples outlined so frequently and touchingly in news and human-interest stories somehow became *our* problem.

My work as a photographer has always involved a total

immersion in other people's lives. Perhaps the time had come to give some consideration to my own.

If this story began in that classroom, and reached crisis point in the doctor's consulting room, what of the intervening twenty years? I see now that a perfectly pleasant, if uneventful, childhood was quickly overturned by a fierce adolescent hunger for life to begin. When I reached the age of eighteen, my parents gave me a Nikon camera. And after leaving college, I set off for India with the camera around my neck. Quite randomly and, as it was to turn out, fortuitously, I passed through Bhopal, where I spent some time documenting a family still struggling for survival after the Union Carbide disaster. The pictures I brought home had won a young photographers' prize and, intoxicated by the notion of photo-journalism, I set forth on this new career without a backward glance. I wanted to be the next Cartier-Bresson. To take my place beside Salgado.

But, though it pains me to confess it, the passing years have brought little but disappointment. Despite this promising beginning, I have languished almost entirely at the margins and learned to my cost how very hard it is, in a world awash with images, to make your mark.

Yet I remain forever hopeful of a change of fortunes, ambition still burning undimmed. Absorbed in a commission, it's as if everything else recedes. Ambient noise falls away. Peripheral vision closes down. On long assignments, I tumble exhausted into sleep, only to find I am struggling to frame my dreams. Sometimes, it is as if a tropical fever is running in my veins. Possessed, on fire, I am helpless in the face of its tyranny. And it's tough on relationships. Tough in particular on Johnny.

Johnny. The second great love of my life. It had been mutual friends, Tamsin and Pete, who introduced us, and my first impression was of someone long-limbed and stylishly dishevelled in a manner that for some reason struck me as rather French. But it was the whimsy of his smile that caught the heart, seeming to reveal an irreverence of spirit that continued, even all these years on, to disarm. I quickly learned that he was a man as easygoing as I was earnest. Certainly his job in advertising indicated someone entirely untroubled by the kind of high-minded ambition that so bedevilled me.

Initially our differences in temperament had amused us. Then, when we began living together, they had become a source of conflict for a while. But over time, a mutual if sometimes grudging admiration had grown again between us. I always knew that it was the security of our relationship that freed me to pursue my career with such commitment, and was grateful for the safe port he offered once the fever receded.

Until one day, quite without warning, everything changed.

*   *   *

A long and particularly absorbing job had just come to an end. An inner London council had commissioned me to document their new pilot project, 'Working for a Better Environment and Healthier Lifestyle'. And somewhat to my surprise, though I'd taken the liberty of broadening it into a rather more controversial and cutting-edge essay on inner-city alienation, they'd remained surprisingly accommodating. After much discussion we'd agreed a final portfolio. There'd even been talk of an exhibition that could tour local libraries and community centres. Privately I'd harboured a secret hope that the project might lead to a book of some kind. That at long last my career might actually be amounting to something of substance.

So there I was, waking as if from a dream, stretching and blinking in the light of day. Focusing at last on my own surroundings. The house was a tip. Piles of paperwork that needed sorting. Bills that must be paid without delay. Unanswered messages from friends. I noticed for the first time there was a chill in the air, that the trees were bare. That winter had crept upon us.

And there, I discovered anew, was Johnny. Beloved Johnny. Boyish of face and long of limb. I was present now in our conversations, ready to take up my share of domestic duties again, eager to resume all social engagements. I remember expressing surprise at how long his hair had grown, to which he had laughed in an unpleasant and puzzlingly sardonic manner. He had seemed quite uncharacteristically out of sorts that morning. But it was only later, when the terrible realisation came to me that I had forgotten it was his birthday, that the panic had set in. Of course I rang immediately in an attempt to make amends, and that evening was sincerely contrite. I was midway through cooking a conciliatory supper when he came in, and an assortment of hastily selected presents were wrapped and waiting on the side. But his manner was abrupt, and nothing I could say appeared to soothe him. He dismissed my abject apologies impatiently. It wasn't *that* that he particularly cared about. It wasn't any *one* thing, he said. The birthday incident was just indicative of a much bigger issue.

'I mean, tell me something, Rose,' he said suddenly. 'Have you any idea what it is I'm working on at the moment?'

He observed me intently, waiting.

'Working on?'

And though I'd rifled quickly through the flotsam and jetsam of recent information relating to his working life, it was undeniably true that shamefully little had come to mind. There'd been that soft drinks campaign. Though that had surely been and gone some time ago.

'There. You see!' The ease of his victory merely serving to further inflame him. 'I was trying to tell you. Just the other day. Only it was perfectly obvious you weren't taking a word of it in.'

I remember being galled to have put up such a feeble performance. I remember suggesting sarcastically that perhaps he should find someone with a nice nine-to-five job. A dentist maybe. Or an accountant. And he had stared at me in silence for some moments. Certainly

I remember a feeling of relief at having clawed back a little ground.

'I suppose . . .' He had run a trembling hand through his hair, before rising in confusion to his feet, an inner agitation appearing to quite overwhelm him. 'I suppose . . .' he had said again, the extent of his disarray quite perplexing me. Then he had turned quickly, distress giving him the face of a stranger. 'I suppose what I'm trying to say is that I've had enough.'

The shock had snapped my head back, as if I'd been dealt a physical blow.

'I see.'

'And I think we should go away somewhere and try and sort it out. Just spend some time together. Either that . . .' he had said with a ferocity I'd never heard in him before, '. . . either that, or call it a day.'

'I see,' I said again, giving him my full and undivided attention now. Listening not just to the words, but to the intonation and even the pauses in between. Outside, the winter winds shrieked a loud lament.

'I'm thirty-six now. You've just turned thirty. We're not kids any more. I mean, where's this relationship actually heading?'

And to my astonishment, I saw that I'd been waiting for this question to be posed for some time now. Here it was at last then. My wake-up call.

2

Ladakh, Cuba, Uruguay. The world at our feet. We pooled our money. I cleared my diary. Johnny's agency gave him a month's unpaid leave. Feeling suddenly free as birds, we agreed, finally, on Vietnam.

In my rucksack somewhere was a postcard Tamsin had given us at a dinner party they gave shortly before we left. She had run after us, urgently waving it to and fro, while behind her a group of old friends had gathered tipsily at the open door, raising glasses and calling last farewells.

'I completely forgot. This came the other day for Pete and me . . .'

Dear friends, it read in a scrawling hand. *Have found Paradise on Earth and may be some time.* It bore a Vietnamese stamp, a name, Xin Chao, and was signed simply 'Bill'.

'You remember him, don't you?'

Johnny had laughed, nodding. 'Guess he had to cut and run. Too many women baying for his blood in this town.'

Though I said nothing, the truth was I also remembered him only too well. I'd first encountered him at one of Tamsin and Pete's famous Christmas parties. Pushing through the crush of guests in a low-backed dress, I'd felt the caress of a stranger's fingers trace my spine, and turned quickly to find a man of striking beauty smiling boldly upon me. Up until then I'd known him by reputation only. He was an actor whose prolific and complex entanglements had become a favourite source of dinner party anecdote amongst our group. And despite the heart leap that he had startled in me – or perhaps because of it – I'd made a point of entirely ignoring him when our paths subsequently crossed, hoping to make it quite clear I was amongst a minority entirely indifferent to his charms.

'Well keep an eye out for him will you?' Tamsin had said. 'He's been gone a while now.' We were huddled close, squinting against the fine drizzle blowing down the street. 'And if you ever get as far as Xin Chao, send him home. We miss him . . .'

I held the card out to her, but she shook her head, already retreating through the rain.

'No, no, take it. You never know when you may need an inside tip.'

Beyond the hotel windows, the traffic noise of Hanoi hummed like tinnitus on the humid, diesel-choked air. Punch-drunk from the long flight, and felled now by heat, I could do no more than loll languidly. For some time I had watched the pallid geckos flick across the ceiling in staccato bursts, half-hypnotised by the blurred wheel of the ceiling fan, and its cool slipstream of displaced air. But Johnny sat at the rickety table, flicking determinedly through guidebooks and unfolding crisp new maps. The elation of arranging the trip had unaccountably waned. Our exchanges were irritably brittle, the unresolved resentments that had brought us here beginning to fester again. He rejected my suggestions, then I in turn rejected his. And the more brisk and purposeful he became, the more inertia paralysed me. With my eyes closed, I listened to the singsong fragments of conversation from the street and the frenzied din of traffic, the weeks before us stretching like a life sentence. *We should never have come*, I thought, humming tunelessly.

'What about Tamsin and Pete's friend?' I opened my eyes again. 'That "paradise on earth" place.'

He sighed. 'Don't be ridiculous.' He hadn't even bothered looking up. 'We don't know anything about it.'

'Exactly.' It took all my reserves of energy to roll over and address him directly, an earthy scent of mildew rising up from the mattress. 'We're on an adventure, Johnny. Isn't that what you do when you're on an adventure?'

He made no reply, absorbed in his pedantic search through the guidebooks. He began to read a passage on the sights of Hanoi, but he'd scarcely begun before I was shaking my head. It sounded everything I wanted to escape. And looking exasperated, he had hunted out the postcard, smoothing it flat, turning to cross-reference it with the guidebook.

'"Designated a National Park in 1993, Xin Chao is an island of quite spectacular natural beauty, boasting unspoilt sandy beaches and dramatic forested inlands. The island has no mains electricity and limited water supplies, which combined with its sheer remoteness and protected status means that tourist facilities remain, for the time being at least, scanty." ' He picked up the postcard again, taking this in.

'Are you really serious? It seems so random.'

'Why not?' I shrugged.

There was a pause while he considered this, then to my surprise he had laughed, the idea seeming to catch him.

'I suppose that's right.' He glanced at me appreciatively, the old recognition at last sparking. 'Why not?'

We took a night train to the south, waking to water-logged paddy fields, then a cab to the coast, where we found ourselves standing, feeling a little foolish, at the water's edge. Confused by our fumbling attempts at Vietnamese, the motorbike taxi had apparently abandoned us in the middle of nowhere. In the shade of beached fishing boats, three fishermen sat cross-legged, mending their nets.

'Xin Chao?' I said tentatively, addressing the eldest member of the group. But he had only shaken his head, looking puzzled.

'Xin Chao?' Johnny repeated. And this time the faces of all three men had instantly lit up, 'Ah, Xin Chao!' they chorused, nodding and smiling, responding with an animated explanation in Vietnamese. When we shook our heads uncomprehendingly, the old man mimed the motion of a boat, and appeared to be urging us to make haste. Then the three men had risen as one, pointing urgently away down the coastline, making encouraging gestures, as if to small children.

So we set off briskly, swinging our rucksacks across our backs, each pressing the other to hurry, though neither of us were sure quite what it was we were hurrying for. Very soon we rounded the headland and came upon a small fishing port. And there, amongst the clustered fishing boats, a ferry – laden with animals and people and preparing to set sail.

'Xin Chao?' Johnny called out, and with much noisy shouting the smiling passengers beckoned us to join them, creating a flurry of good-humoured commotion as they rose to make space on the crowded deck. We'd scarcely taken our places before the anchor was hauled from the sea, and the boat had set sail.

As the island came at last into view, I took a photograph of Johnny squeezed between a tethered goat and a wicker cage of chickens, a glimpse of the looming harbour just beyond his right shoulder.

'One day you'll look at this, and remember our grand adventure.' I was struggling to find focus, the deck shifting treacherously beneath my feet.

'I think it's more likely,' he said, eyeing my battered old Nikon, 'that I'll look at it and remember there were three of us in this relationship.'

At the rickety pier, people and animals had streamed on to dry land as if from a disembarking Noah's Ark. We bought pineapples from a small stall and headed out of town, following the dusty dirt track past mangrove trees, whose exposed roots made it appear they were wrenching themselves free.

After a short while, we came to a clearing and stopped abruptly, finding ourselves gazing along the length of a beach where fine white sand shelved gently into clear turquoise water. Windblown palm trees skirted its length, and between them the thatched roofs of scattered huts on stilts. It seemed a paradise so absurdly Platonic in its perfection that we turned to one another laughing at its preposterous implausibility.

An elderly man approached through the trees speaking eagerly, his elfin face alight with expectation.

'I think he's trying to sell you a massage.'

'Maybe later,' I tried to mime, but the man stood his ground, smiling hopefully.

'Listen, you have a massage and I'll go and sort out a room.' Johnny lifted the rucksacks one across each shoulder and set off slowly up the beach, while the old man shook out a mat for me and I lay down.

Under his strong hands, the little bones had rolled and ached, the tendons singing out as if flesh were being moulded into clay. The clamour of sensations shut out the external world, time moving in strange cycles of pain, until there came an unpleasant sensation of fingers pressing into my ears. I raised an arm as the pressure became intolerable, but still his fingers bore in. My eardrums felt huge in my head, great bulbous balloons that pressed against my skull. Then a burst of light as the pressure was released and I opened my eyes and sat up. Before me the translucent sea and distant mountains sprung newly minted, and all about me the fine song of birds whistled a hallelujah chorus.

I was heading, rubber limbed, towards the huts, when Johnny's angry shout brought me to an abrupt halt.

'Fuck! Fuck! Fuck!' His distraught figure appeared on the veranda of one of the huts close by. 'Someone's stolen all our money! Everything! Gone! Passports! Plane tickets!'

I scanned wildly, expecting to see robbers running away through the trees.

'I went to unpack our stuff and the whole lot had just completely vanished . . .'

'My camera?'

'No,' he said tersely, swinging it towards me. 'That's the only thing of value left.'

I seized it, holding it gratefully.

'It must have been on the ferry. Somehow, amongst all the people and animals . . .' He was pacing up and down, a hand shielding his brow as he tried to puzzle it out. 'Fuckers!' He slammed the wall.

'Well . . . We'll just have to . . . We'll just have to call home. See if my parents can send some money as soon as possible.' His face expressed incredulity at my slow-wittedness.

'We're in a national park. Remember?'

I shook my head, smiling stupidly.

'No telephone masts. No reception.'

'Okay . . .' My thoughts turned sluggishly, the massage seeming to have loosened key neural connections.

He stood with hands on hips. 'No phone service,' he said in a strained voice. 'No bank for anyone to send anything to anyway. So no money to pay for our room. Or to get us off the island. I mean, maybe the British consulate would bail us out, but since we can't get back to the mainland to ask, it's entirely academic really . . .' He shrugged.

'Christ . . .' I closed my eyes, and sat down heavily, my legs folding of their own accord.

'So much for your great adventure then . . .' He walked away down the beach, kicking up angry sprays of sand.

Though the water was still limpid and the sun un-dimmed, I had the oddest sensation we'd just dropped in free fall off the edge of the world.

We reported the theft to the lone policeman who inhabited a corrugated iron hut not far from the jetty; he had expressed surprise at the theft, promising to look into it as a matter of some urgency. At least we hoped, in the elaborate gesticulations and nods that passed between us, that that was what had been said. In particular we had been at pains to impress on him that we had international flights to catch in just over three weeks' time. And though there was nothing to do but wait, apprehension now cast a long shadow over the loveliness of our surroundings. At least, we tried to comfort one another, our room remained secure for the time being, and our handful of change would buy food and drink for a few days yet. And there was always the camera. If all else failed, we would have to sell it. Though it was a long shot, there was also an outside chance that Bill might remain somewhere on the island. In the afternoon we went for a stroll, hopefully scanning the travellers who scattered the beaches, or hung out in the bar by the harbour. It was a small place. If he were still here, it could only be a matter of time before we stumbled upon him.

The sky was a bluer blue here. Even the cloud formations were different. We lay side by side in mute contemplation. Then Johnny began to laugh in disbelief.

'What?'

'Us . . . shipwrecked. How are we ever going to get out of this one?' He covered his face. 'Jesus wept. If Bill doesn't turn up soon, or this policeman can't help us, *we are* going to have to do *something*, you know.'

An international flight to catch, jobs to get back to, a whole life waiting to be resumed. We both lie in solemn contemplation. A micro hum of insect wings.

The intermittent notes of tropical birdsong. The dilemma hanging unanswerably. I reached for my book, my only desire to lose myself amongst its pages. But claustrophobia pressed upon me now, the blue sea and sky seeming to contain us like a gilded cage.

Yet as the first day flowed into the next, the heat soon produced an anaesthetising torpor in us both. As the temperatures climbed, the fleshy smell of the earth would rise up to scent the felty air, and all anxieties would recede before the sun's onslaught. The hours would vanish in a daze of reading, swimming and dozing. In this limbo of waiting, perhaps *because* of this limbo, an undeniably easeful drifting was stealing upon us; an indolent unfurling of night into day, of day back into night. And like a dislocated joint resuming its socket, we found we were once again united. We had lost everything except each other. And in this newly congenial spirit, somehow it seemed that though one day might be closing behind without resolution, another would shortly be dawning in its stead, filled anew with hope.

One evening, we visited the local temple and lit incense. The shadows were comforting and we sat for a while in silence, watching the fragrant smoke spiral upwards. Already it was hard to remember quite how our days had been so urgently and meaningfully structured in that old life so far away across the globe.

Every day we went to visit the policeman. Often we found him fast asleep, with his legs propped up on the desk and his peaked cap covering his face. When Johnny cleared his throat, he would wake with a start, leaping to his feet, and fumbling to return the cap to his head with a hasty formality. But he never had any new developments to report. We might have requested he contact the mainland for us. We might have thrown ourselves upon his mercy. There were all manner of things we would like to have asked of him. But he spoke not a word of English and we no Vietnamese. Days passed. Almost a week. We were well and truly adrift.

All that week, we'd haunted the harbour bar, hopeful that our luck might change and we would stumble across Bill. I had a vision of him turning from his table to greet us. Laughing incredulously as we explained our plight. Reaching unhesitatingly into his pockets for generous fistfuls of money.

One night we fell into conversation with a group of travellers. Fuelled by rice wine, the evening had grown progressively more exuberant as rounds were ordered and newcomers drifted over to join our table. An amusing conversation with Voon Wong, a student from Hong Kong, had given way to a heated debate with Yuri, an Israeli lecturer in history, only to be interrupted by an eccentric monologue from Brad, an Australian marine biologist on sabbatical for a year. There was an instant kinship in having journeyed from different corners of the world, leaving behind modern lives, to find ourselves washed up together on a remote and primitive island. And this spirit of kinship cast an enchantment on the evening, firing all of us with a buccaneering swagger at our fearlessness. The conversation had turned to a night dive that was taking place the following evening, and at some stage, amidst the gales of laughter and drifting smoke, Johnny and I had made an impetuous decision to spend the last of our money and join them. After all, we had agreed airily, who could possibly know what solutions tomorrow might bring?

Late in the swirl and press of people, I'd fallen into conversation with Eugenia. I'd noticed her earlier, sitting at the outskirts of the group, looking on with a gravely beautiful face. She was nursing a broken heart, she confided in a husky Spanish accent. A brief love affair with a fellow traveller had just come to an untimely and unexpected end. 'He was English like you,' she said. I was nodding sympathetically, when it dawned on me exactly what she was about to tell me. His name was Bill, she continued sorrowfully. But he had left the island at the beginning of the week and now she would never see him again. Then we'd both lapsed into a pensive silence and Eugenia had wiped away a furtive tear.

I'd broken the news of Bill's departure to Johnny as we made our way home through the darkened mangrove swamp. 'Bang goes that rescue plan then,' he'd said, staggering a little unsteadily on his feet. 'Thoughtless bugger ... Look's like we'll have to sell that bloody camera of yours then.'

On the easterly breeze I felt the sea's great billowing

expanse hidden by the night. It's hard to account for what possessed me now, but in a few bounds I had crossed the springy sands and flung the camera far into the darkness beyond. Moments later came a subdued and satisfying splash. The last sustaining thread from which we dangled had been severed. Perhaps it was the rice wine burning in our bellies, but the odd thing was that our laughter was the laughter of a quite unexpected and soaring elation.

That night Johnny came to me, looming out of the darkness, with the torch glowing in one hand.

'I've crossed the wild seas to ravish you, fair maiden,' he growled in a gruff pirate's voice, his mouth so close that his breath burnt the inside of my ear. He nuzzled my neck, pinning my arms, as I struggled to escape, the unbearable writhing belly laughter of being tickled overtaking me.

'Get OFF me, you horrible great *oaf*,' I wrenched myself free, falling to the floor, where my head lodged awkwardly, too weak to move.

'For I want you to be the mother of my child. What say you, lady? Hey? What say you?' The torch clattered away across the pitted floor, casting Halloween shadows beyond the bright cone of its illumination.

'Never,' I cried, limp-limbed, wiping away the tears that had run across my cheeks and into my hair.

'Ahh, you coward,' he scoffed in his pantomime voice. 'You modern women are a lily-livered bunch.'

My voice rising indignantly. 'You're so full of bullshit.'

'Oh, you think so, do you?'

'Yes! Yes, I do actually.'

'Try me then,' he said, unexpectedly resuming his own voice.

In the darkness, just the catch of our breath and the glitter of eyes and teeth. The air between us quite still. I felt for the packet of condoms that lay beneath the bed.

'Well, you see these?' I held them in the torchlight. 'And you see this?' I reached out towards the gleam of the penknife lying close by, prising open the little scissors hidden inside and snipping each little foil packet in two, the fragments falling away into the velvety darkness. 'Who's the coward now?'

He said nothing, eyes blazing in the half-light.

'You're all talk, Johnny Mitchell.'

In his astonishment he appeared to have entirely forgotten our game. I shrugged the straps of my dress from my shoulders.

'It's up to you. Take it or leave it . . .'

And as we tumbled, entwined, skin against skin, we were serious now and intent.

'Scared?' he asked afterwards, watching me move softly about the room. I leaned down to untangle the discarded clothes, but stopped to hold his gaze for a moment before I had to look away, heart skittering.

'What's to be scared of?' I said lightly.

*   *   *

The birds were squabbling over scraps from the morning catch, and already a heat haze was rippling at the end of the pier. Jacques, the French-Canadian dive master sat at our centre, writing down names and taking money, his bracelets clattering and sliding against his sunburnt arms. There was a great show of carelessness and *joie de vivre* amongst us all as we assembled again; backs were slapped, cigarettes lobbed into outstretched hands, a teasing and flirtatious banter thrown breezily to and fro.

Then a clatter of squawks brought all conversation to an abrupt halt as a cockerel burst from the kitchen, pursued by a young girl who clapped her hands as he lopped comically between the tables, splayed claws beating the earth, beak stretched wide in frantic alarm. We raised our feet as he charged beneath the long trestle table, but Jacques, with a cigarette burning nonchalantly in the corner of his mouth, had coolly leaned down and seized him up by the scruff of the neck. 'You want to eat here – first you must catch.' He was brandishing the poor creature aloft, his words half drowned by the wild whistling and clucking chicken imitations.

Jacques had dropped out of merchant banking to travel the world, picking up work here and there, before moving on. But he had been on Xin Chao for a while now, he said. 'Too long, man . . . Lots of people come, everything change. Every time, the same thing.' He drawled his words, the torpid intonation suggesting a man enviably untrammelled. In a few weeks he planned to move on again, probably heading for Cambodia, to a series of remote islands off the coast of Sihanoukville. 'People keep telling me they're worth checking out. Nothing there apparently. You pick up a vibe, you know. Makes you curious.' He shrugged. There was something in this gypsy insouciance that triggered a desire in each of us to impress, vying with one another for his approbation. Even Eugenia was newly vivacious in his presence, while Johnny set forth his best travel stories, acting out the bits that might be hard to follow in English. At the head of the table, Jacques listened while he counted the money, nodding sagely, rewarding him sometimes with a guffaw of laughter.

Yet despite the good humour of the gathering, I was troubled by a creeping trepidation. Perhaps it was concern that we were so rashly spending the last of our money in this way. Almost certainly it was regret at having so impetuously disposed of my camera. Last night we had been carried on a spirit of reckless abandon, that today had shrunk away without trace. Behind the counter, the wife of the bar's proprietor was feeding her small son, talking to him all the while in a lilting singsong. For some reason the two of them kept drawing my eye, and though the conversation at our table was boisterous, increasingly I let it break about me. There was something in the woman's delight I was trying to fathom. Seeing me staring at her son, she smiled proudly and nodded quizzically. *You too?*

No! I shook my head hastily, emphatically – *no children*.

She cocked her head. 'Soon,' she offered sympathetically in broken English. *She thinks my time is running out*, I realised, amused. It wouldn't cross her mind that I would have *chosen* to have reached thirty without having had children. There'd be little point in trying to tell her about my demanding career as a photographer, even if my skills at sign language stretched that far.

'Maybe one day,' I nodded politely.

She turned back to the boy, wiping the traces of food from his face.

Maybe even now, I thought uneasily, reluctant to recall our unprotected coupling in the Halloween shadows. Loath to consider its possible consequences.

Beyond us the sea sparkled. As a child I had often walked beside the North Sea. The sucking grey water had been terrifying up close. This sea was a different entity all together. This sea was the water of Eden, the colour of joy. But even here, as the lead weights of the diving belt bore you downwards, the blood warmth would drain quickly away, the great mass of water growing in weight on every side. It was this weight of water that preoccupied me now. How very easily new life might be snuffed out.

'I'm not going to come tonight.'

The assembled table turned in surprise. I couldn't look Jacques in the eye, sick at heart to have abdicated so feebly from the competition for his approval. Eugenia seized my hand.

'Oh pleeease, Rose. You must . . .'

'Are you all right?' Johnny was frowning.

'I'm tired, that's all. Think I'll just crash out early. But

I'll be with you all in spirit.' I glanced quickly around the group.

'Suit yourself,' Jacques said shrugging. 'I hope you won't regret. They make great wildlife discoveries in Vietnam still. Someone found a whole new kind of fish the other day. Who knows what might be waiting for us down in those dark seas tonight . . .'

Eugenia shrieked in delighted terror. 'You cannot be serious!'

'Hey, did anyone else hear this?' One of the Australians addressed us. 'Apparently the sharks round here have this special thing for the Spanish? Go completely crazy for them I'm told.'

'Ah well, then they're smarter than some men I know.' Eugenia laughed, sweeping back her hair, and darting a quick look at Jacques.

Their raillery continued, anticipation quickening at the shared adventure that lay ahead, while I, an outsider now, sat looking on. They were celebrating their immortality, revelling in having no one but themselves to consider. And it was only so very recently that I had shared this carelessness. It was alarming to be slipping inexorably onwards, tugged by these unsettling new currents. Jacques threw an arm around me.

'Think it over, huh? Life is for living you know.'

But my eyes were fixed upon the Vietnamese woman who had lifted up her son now and was dancing with him cheek to cheek, enraptured.

*   *   *

I woke with a start, as if having fallen from a great height. The plink plink of birdsong. The distant weight of sea. And beside me a space. No Johnny. I flicked the light on the travel clock. One o'clock. They should be back by now. I pushed myself upright to look through silhouetted palm trees at the glittering sea.

The torch, when I found it, flickered and went out. But somewhere in the rucksacks there were spare batteries. Like a blind woman, I searched our bags in the darkness, feeling familiar textures under my fingertips. Soft clothes, slippery book covers, but no cold metal. I worked my way methodically, the feeling of urgency pressing upon me in the dark. Then my fingers found the spiky scar of a zip in the inner recesses of Johnny's bag, a hidden place, and ran it open. Within its deep embrace, my fingers slid across the smooth fat sheen of documents. All our money, passports and air tickets, evidently stashed here for safekeeping and then forgotten. I sat trying to catch my breath, unable to quite take in the sheer opulent weight of this unexpected discovery in my hands, before a joyful and incredulous laugh burst from me. And then I remembered Johnny, and anxiety forced me up again. No time to be wasted.

I dressed quickly, and slipped down the wooden stairs, hastening through the trees to the sea. Following the curve of the beach I kept walking, waiting for the jetty to come into view. Under the night sky, I saw that there was in fact no need for the torch. The moon and stars lit my way, blazing above me in the dark void.

Occasionally a shooting star trailed before me, its fiery thread glimmering before almost simultaneously vanishing again. The rhythm of my gait was reassuring, filling the night with purposeful movement. Forwards, forwards. At last the jetty. And moored at the end, Jacques' boat. They must be back then. Halfway down I saw huddled silhouettes, and the flicker of an oil lamp. Drawing nearer still, I began to catch their voices, urgent and low, a seaweedy tang on the air. And now I was running, the jetty shifting queasily beneath my feet.

'Johnny! *Johnny!*'

He was sitting at the jetty's edge, stooped over, hawking and coughing into the sea. The huddled group broke ranks to admit me. In the half-light his wet hair looked like blood cascading down his face. I threw my arms around him, the damp rubber of his wetsuit clammy under my hands.

'What happened?'

He seemed too dazed to speak. I rounded on them. The faces that clustered about him were lost in shadow, but I could hear Eugenia sobbing quietly amongst them. Jacques stepped forward, a placating hand outstretched.

'We dived down to an underwater cave. And Johnny lost his sense of direction. He had a – you know, a – panic attack. And his diving-buddy . . .' he glanced quickly towards Eugenia, an edge to his voice '. . . was not beside him when he needed her.'

One of the Australians speaks up in a shaky tone. 'Used up nearly all his air thrashing round. Then Jacques got him out. Saved his bloody life, I reckon.'

I pulled him to me, holding him fiercely. 'Christ, Johnny. Are you okay?'

He nodded mutely, but I could feel him quaking, his teeth chattering like a cartoon skeleton.

'Just take it easy, my friend.' Jacques crouched beside him, putting a hand on his shoulder.

'We need to get him to the shore. Warm him up . . .' Eugenia was shivering so violently she could barely get the words out.

Then Johnny leaned sharply over and retched. A spew of phlegm hit the water, before he coughed and straightened, wiping his mouth. 'Christ,' he said miserably. 'Talk about your life flashing in front of you . . .' He turned to look at me and even in the darkness, I could see how pale he was, eye sockets like blank hollows beneath his brow bone.

'Come on,' I said shakily, helping him to his feet. Wondering what on earth we were doing here, playing at playing, all these millions of miles from home. A longing to return coming over me like the onset of flu. Eugenia was still sobbing, the sound juddering oddly through her rattling teeth, and one of the Australian boys put a comforting arm around her as we made our way slowly down the rickety jetty.

'I sorry, Johnny. I so sorry,' she moaned, reaching out a conciliatory hand to touch him.

'It's fine. Really. Don't worry about it,' he said, flinching so sharply at her touch that she began to cry more bitterly still.

*   *   *

Back in our bamboo hut, now warm and dry, with a shot of whisky or two inside him, Johnny fell into a deep sleep. Then somewhere around midday he emerged again, stretching and smiling. He observed me benevolently, surveying the sea and sky with relish. Life had been renewed.

'Sit down, close your eyes!' I instructed imperiously. And obediently, he had complied.

'Hold out your hands!' And again he obeyed, smiling in amusement.

'What do you most want in all the world?' I asked, triumphantly dangling a pillowcase heavy with all our worldly goods; the golden keys of home, high above his outstretched hands. He smiled more broadly still, his eyes tightly closed, savouring the moment.

'I told you,' he said, flexing his fingers, apparently ready to take at last the weight of his heart's desire. His voice was rapt. 'Our baby.'

3

Melancholy grey skies greeted us in England. Together with a wind that cut like a blade, people running before it with heads down and closed faces. The short daylight hours seemed only to contain the ugly rasping of rooks and crows.

And there was ambition, waiting for me as if I'd never been away, falling about my shoulders with the familiarity of an old coat. Since photo-journalism seemed to be a dwindling art, I could see now that concentrating on portraiture was going to be the only way to rescue this flagging career of mine. And with renewed energy I set about chasing commissions and reviving old contacts. I was so immersed, that the arrival of my period a few days after our return struck me only as a lucky escape. There would be no stolen body, no loss of self. My sovereignty felt newly sweet. It wasn't that I didn't want children. Rather that I wasn't quite ready to face them just yet. Though without needing to discuss the matter, Johnny and I threw aside all contraceptive measures now. Our reconciliation was implicitly premised on opening the door to this new possibility. I understood that well enough. But quick calculations reassured me how little, when the time came to face it, the whole business need impact on my projects. After all, there would be no point in telling anyone I worked with once I was pregnant. Not until I really had to. Then there would be a brief hospital visit for the birth, and I'd be back behind the camera again.

The thought of the birth always triggered the uneasy memory of the alarming biology film we'd watched at school. Yet each month the arrival of another period signalled that there would be no need to face anything just yet. No need to step back, stand down, or make compromises of any kind. I was running fleet of foot beside my contemporaries still, androgynous and uncompromised.

One day I came across photographs in a Sunday magazine bearing the by-line Richard Makepeace. PEOPLE OF SOWETO, the headline ran. I observed the pictures carefully, scanning with a covetous eye. A series of striking street portraits. By turns poignant and wryly amusing. I distantly recalled Richard Makepeace's name. He'd come to see me for advice after he graduated. Someone had suggested he talk to me, and I'd shown him around my studio while he asked diligent questions and nodded attentively at my suggestions. I'd been flattered by his assumption that I had wisdom worth imparting. Now here he was, fully launched with a prestigious book about to be published, and this magazine spread to publicise it. I thought of the bread-and-butter bookings that littered my diary: the catalogue work; the corporate commissions; the minor celebrity portraits. What had become of the book I had always planned? Far from running fleet of foot, I saw I was in actual fact now languishing some way behind.

'But surely that's the beauty of portraiture?' Gabriel had leaned back in his chair, scratching thoughtfully. 'You can photograph virtually anyone you set your mind to. People in the public eye need you as much as you need them.'

Tamsin was serving Sunday lunch to a noisily chaotic gathering of friends.

'For instance . . .'

He rummaged through the pile of Tamsin and Pete's newspapers that overflowed the recycling box, until he found what he was looking for and handed it to me, indicating a small article on the front page. I took it, frowning curiously, and read a brief account of a forth-coming visit to Britain by the Dalai Lama.

'See!' he laughed at my puzzled face, at the self-evident simplicity of his proposal. Several friends stopped to listen, scanning the article curiously over my shoulder. 'Spotted it yesterday.'

'What? Photograph the Dalai Lama!' The voices as one. A ripple of amusement around the table. I pushed the paper away, smiling with them.

'Very funny.'

But Gabriel only shrugged, unperturbed. 'Give me one good reason why not?'

'It isn't that simple.'

'Isn't it?'

I stared at him, exasperated at his wilful naivety. As a

documentary film-maker he clearly considered this to be his specialist subject. And despite myself an undeniably seductive concept was forming in my mind's eye: a portrait series of contemporary figureheads, whose reflected glory in turn illuminated me.

'David Beckham!' Johnny offered, when I tentatively tried the idea out loud.

'The Queen,' Tamsin laughed, passing round more wine. 'Pete's mother would like that.'

'Nelson Mandela.'

'What about Bob Dylan?'

There were groans and cheers, a fierce debate breaking out with loyalties and counter loyalties being declared on every side.

'Great photographers get there by aligning themselves with the great,' Gabriel said, as though he'd read my thoughts. 'Be bold. Think big.'

Still I said nothing, turning the notion over, while the argument rumbled on around us. He tore the story out.

'Anyway. What's to lose?' He yawned and stretched, before tossing it dismissively across the table.

It was some days later when, on the whim of a moment, I finally dialled the organisation mentioned in the article. Just passing time. It would at the very least amuse Gabriel when I next saw him. The man who took the call confirmed the Dalai Lama's imminent trip to Britain and listened courteously before advising I put my request for a portrait sitting in writing. His voice was as light and melodic as a flute. He spelt his name carefully, Tsering

Tashi, and asked that I address the letter to him. He was the Dalai Lama's British envoy.

'Are you really saying there's a possibility?' I asked, astonished at his matter of factness.

'The only problem is the time factor. As you would expect, His Holiness has many requests, and his commitments are most numerous. But anything is possible. His Holiness considers each one equally.'

So I had sat down and composed a careful letter.

I'm a photographer in the process of putting together a fine-art collection of photographic portraits, 'Twenty-first Century Heroes and Icons', that will represent a diverse and thought-provoking cross-section of contemporary figureheads drawn from the arts, science, sport and religion.

A percentage of profits will be donated to Opportunity UK, a leading children's charity that provides mentoring for vulnerable children.

Then I sent it off. Like a message in a bottle. And the unexpectedly promising nature of the conversation spurred me on. I plundered Gabriel's contact book.

'Well, Camera Press has a large archive of the Queen. You could always negotiate with them to use one for your book.'

'Oh, no. You see, the idea is that all the photographs will be taken by me.'

'She tends to do lots of sittings for paintings. Not

so many for photographs. Can't think of one since the Golden Jubilee in fact.'

'I see . . .'

'But write to the Queen's Private Secretary, here – at Buckingham Palace – outlining the book. The more detail the better. It would very much depend on the type of project you see. I mean, no harm in asking is there?'

The wedding was an impromptu register office affair. We bought the flowers on the way, from a wind-blown stall on the corner, and I wore a charity shop dress I'd never found the right occasion for before. Johnny looked rakishly handsome, though his hand was damp when I took it in mine for the exchange of vows. His father came from Hove. My parents all the way from Durham. Tamsin and Pete were our witnesses, and Gabriel arrived too late for the ceremony, but gave a very witty speech in the hotel bar we all stumbled into a little while later. Tamsin, now heavily pregnant with her first child, had even remembered confetti. Like many of our co-habiting friends, she had expressed surprise that we were bothering to make our relationship official in this day and age. But though I struggled to articulate it, there was something decidedly liberating in relinquishing the need to keep life's options forever open. A poignancy in forsaking all others to set off hand in hand, along a path you knew perfectly well to be both outmoded and perilous.

At some point in the drunken festivities, Johnny's father had stood up and offered a toast to Johnny's dead mother.

'She'd 've been very proud of you, boy. Very proud indeed,' and we'd all raised our glasses, instantly moist-eyed and maudlin.

'Well done, well done. Finally made an honest man of the old bugger,' he'd said later, winking conspiratorially at me, pumping my hand before gathering his coat and hat, and hastening off to catch the last train. Then he'd turned and come back again, emotion seeming quite involuntarily to overcome him.

'Not long before we hear the patter of tiny Mitchell feet then!' And seizing me in a fierce embrace, he'd planted a damp kiss on either cheek, before turning back to the door with a curious dance-like step.

It had been a charming affair, we both agreed afterwards. Surprisingly traditional in its own chaotic way.

Tamsin's baby had arrived shortly afterwards. A little boy perpetually at her breast. I'd gone to see her once or twice, but she'd been distracted, scarcely seeming to register the gifts I laid beside her, or my attempts to engage her in conversation. A few weeks later, a politely worded letter of refusal arrived from Buckingham Palace. But from Free Tibet, there was still no word. And at some point, quite imperceptibly, things began to change. Somehow the weeks were drifting into months. And the feeling of relief when yet another period came was receding, while in its place grew a distinct restlessness that this motherhood thing, this otherness, was inexplicably eluding me. I found myself vexed to have given permission and yet to receive no result. And by some curious process of evolution, trepidation was gradually metamorphosing into something strangely akin to wanting. Indeed undeniably *identical* to wanting. And the sense of a baby which had been something entirely unvisualised, was paradoxically beginning to be made vivid at last by its very absence.

Increasingly the mediocrity of the commissions that clustered my diary filled me with a deepening impatience. And when still no word came from the Dalai Lama's office, impatience became an agitation. As the months gathered behind us without result, I was overwhelmed by the feeling that there must be something more than this. Not simply because the actual doing of my work was unrewarding. But more painfully that it continually faded away, like footprints in sand, time rendering it no more than a sneeze in the great grand scheme of the world. We had enjoyed an extended adolescence, spanning, as it had for so many of our generation, much of our twenties, and for Johnny half his thirties too. The time to commit to something of substance was patently long overdue.

For the first time I found myself watching passing babies with a distinctly covetous eye. And caught in this half-life, I was struggling to reconcile this new sensibility to the old, because at some indefinable stage I appeared to have segued from male into female. As if from night into day. Apparently from nowhere, an astonishing revelation came to me one day that the woman's terrible howling in that school film all those years ago could be seen not as torment, but as primitive celebration. An exultant acknowledgement of the life-force. And the thought so astounded me with its complete reversion of everything that had hitherto defined my views on childbirth, that I momentarily lost my balance and had to sit down to absorb it.

Then Tamsin, on the verge of returning to work, quite unexpectedly announced she was pregnant again. Pete was furious, she said, shrugging rebelliously. As a picture editor, she'd often put jobs my way and I had been looking forward to her return to the world we shared. It was she who had given me my first professional commission, our friendship slowly growing out of the various projects we worked on together. We had seemed partners in crime.

And now, suddenly, not just Tamsin, but a veritable host of friends were producing babies with enviable ease all about me. There was a flurry of visits to greet wizened newborns, swaddled like sugar almonds. Once or twice the mysterious creature had been thrust into my arms while I sat in secret thrilled alarm until it was lifted ceremoniously from me again. But Johnny remained always reassuringly phlegmatic. I'd only recently come off the pill, he reminded me. It took time for the body to adjust, to rebalance itself. And Tamsin too was quick to dismiss my worries, urging patience. It *will* happen, she said consolingly. But increasingly, as I watched her slowly swell all over again, I doubted her.

So I bought ovulation kits and we made love according to their metronome tick. I marked the day in my diary, and overpowered Johnny with desire as the day drew near. The new spring, summer and autumn of our love-making, my passions entirely moderated by this calendar. At first it gave us vigour and focus. Johnny was taken aback at my new ardour, at the fire with which it flowered for just a brief few days each month, at the chill of the fallow period that followed so closely behind.

Then very quickly, the ticking became oppressively insistent, a monthly imperative that must be obeyed. One night, when Johnny rang to say he would have to work late, I indignantly reminded him that he had to return home or risk missing this month's fleeting window of opportunity. And though he dutifully complied, our love-making was bleakly mechanical. We didn't speak afterwards, as if we were prostitute and client whose coupling was no more than chilly pragmatism. We lay with our backs to one another, until after a moment Johnny got up again. I heard the thud of the fridge door. I heard him moving quietly about the flat. And I lay alone, for what seemed a long time, before sleep finally came.

*　　*　　*

Yet still the months were falling before us. Another six months flashed past. Six stars marking ovulation in my diary that came to nothing. Then another six, like blurred bridges on a motorway.

'I'm worried.' I'd finally confessed in an offhand way one day.

Johnny was taking his morning shower, half-obscured by clouds of steam.

'You're what?'

'*Worried*. I'm worried.'

'I can't . . .' He struggled hopelessly with the shower controls. 'You know I can't HEAR you when I'm in the shower.'

He craned his head towards me, away from the thunderous water, grimacing as shampoo frothed across his eyes and into his mouth.

'We need to do something about this not getting pregnant business.' Though even as I said it, I was wondering why I had chosen such an inopportune moment. As if secreting the issue away would avoid promoting it to one of significance.

'That's fine, darling. Call Doctor What's-his-name. Go and talk to him . . .'

'No, Johnny. *We*. We need to do something.'

He was making darting gestures at his face, as if bees were swarming there.

'Christ!' He sought blindly for a towel, snatching at air. 'Do we have to have this conversation now, Rose? Can't this wait till I —'

'No, fine. Fine. It's down to me then. My problem. You're busy.'

And propelled at last into action, I finally sat down to make the call.

The consulting room was a sunless, dispiriting room. While the doctor called up our notes on the computer, we scanned the drab leaflets pinned to the noticeboard, and shifted our feet restlessly on the worn linoleum. I'd always prided myself on scarcely having been here. In fact if it hadn't been for all those years on the contraceptive pill, I'm not sure I would ever have stepped through his door. And the irony of this had not been lost on us. How neat it would be, we had jokingly agreed while we waited, if the effects of that pill could now simply be reversed to produce the converse effect.

The doctor sat with hands in the prayer position, fingertips resting on the bridge of his nose, listening closely to our story. I'd been hoping for no more than a quick reassurance and dismissal, but he appeared to be taking our worries rather too seriously for comfort. Trying to avoid looking at the gruesome steel implements laid out on the side table, and the utilitarian bed with its scratchy paper covering, I focused my eyes fixedly on his grave face. The nurse would take a sample of my blood, while Johnny must take a specimen jar of his sperm to a nearby hospital.

'Then come and see me next week and we'll discuss the results,' he'd said in farewell, standing up abruptly and leaning forward to swing open the door and expel us.

Rain had streaked the windscreen, rivulets of water splitting the lights of the city into vivid mosaics, and all that filled the angry silence was the judder of windscreen wipers and the low humming of the car radio. Johnny sighed deeply, tapping time against the steering wheel.

'Don't make this into a huge issue, Rose.'

'It's just one little sample . . .'

'I just don't think it's necessary.'

'So you keep saying. But why? Why isn't it "necessary"?'

I rested my head against the cold window, watching the passing cars, like gliding capsules taking their inhabitants purposefully forth on smoothly untroubled trajectories. As the lights changed to red we had slid to a halt, though Johnny kept staring fixedly ahead.

'I just don't think it is.'

'Oh, I see. Sorry. Of course! Because being infallible, any problem must be down to me?'

He turned at last to address me. 'Because when Janey and I were living together, she got pregnant once. That's why.' Then he looked quickly away again, chewing his lip.

In the early days of our relationship, just the very mention of Janey's name could be enough to provoke an argument. But it was years since I'd given her any thought. Now here she was again, dimpling and bobbing loathsomely before us.

'Right . . .'

He appeared as nonplussed as I at her abrupt return. Then a car horn jolted him into life and he struggled with the gearstick, lurching us forward once more. After a moment he'd said something so softly, I had to lean close to catch it. 'It was a huge thing at the time. We were still students you see. She had to have an abortion.'

'Right . . .' The indignation was vanishing now, like air from a puncture wound. 'And you didn't ever think it worth mentioning before?'

It was after this unwelcome confession that he finally agreed to provide a sample, more as a sop to my hurt feelings than anything else. I had offered to take it to the hospital, consoling myself that though a check on Johnny's fertility might now be academic, it was at least a gesture of solidarity. Our instructions had been to keep the sample warm and get it there within the hour. I had driven with it trapped fast in the crook of my arm, and somehow this reminder that the jar held life had made the mission a surprisingly poignant one. At the hospital dispatch, I had even experienced a distinctly protective pang as I handed it over to the stranger behind the counter.

A week later we had returned for our results, and waited while our GP rifled ruminatively through the laboratory paperwork, as if hopeful of stumbling across new figures that might throw an all-together more optimistic light on matters. It didn't take an expert in body language to see he had bad news for us. Privately, I had already made my own diagnosis and narrowed it down to either an undiagnosed infection in my youth, or a tragically premature menopause. Would Johnny stand by me once my culpability was officially confirmed? I glanced quickly at him, but his expression remained inscrutable. At last the doctor cleared his throat and made uneasy eye contact.

'Yours . . .' he had said, glancing quickly at me, 'yours seem fine. These tests tell us you are ovulating normally. But yours . . .' he turned now to Johnny. 'Well, the results are not good. Not good at all, I'm afraid. According to these figures the quality and mobility of your sperm is very poor.' Like pistol cracks hard in my ear; the jubilation of relief, snapped out by guilt, crashing entirely under the weight of shock. 'To have any chance of conceiving I am going to have to refer you for specialist help.'

'But Johnny, Johnny's fathered a child once. Years ago, with someone else,' I said, bewildered.

The doctor had shrugged delicately, glancing away. 'Well, it is not for me to —'

It is not for me to say that it could not have been your child. That you were cuckolded.

Out of the corner of my eye, I saw Johnny nod slowly, absorbing his implication as clearly as if he'd voiced it.

As we stepped outside, Johnny had stumbled against me. I turned to take his arm, but he scarcely seemed to notice, walking mechanically, like a sleepwalker, his face a blank mask of shock. He appeared entirely lost to me, and I could only guess, since he couldn't or wouldn't speak, what the nature of the inward blow must be; core notions of potency, of virility, of manhood even, in disarray. Yet to broach these issues felt an unwarranted intrusion. One that risked diminishing him still further. I linked my arm through his and as we walked together in silence there had been something defining in the moment. Already I could see that though the diagnosis might implicate us both, it would also simultaneously divide us. My reprieve had been earned at his expense. After a moment or two he had gathered himself, and embraced me briefly, with face half-averted, before going off to work.

PART TWO

Row, row, row your boat, gently down the stream,
Merrily, merrily, merrily, life is but a dream!

Rock, rock, rock your boat, gently to and fro,
If you see a crocodile, don't forget to scream!

Traditional children's song

4

And so here we now sit, Johnny and I, before this consultant our doctor has referred us to, as he outlines a new treatment for male infertility.

'ICSI,' he says, enunciating carefully. 'An acronym for intracytoplasmic sperm injection,' the hard-edged language of science momentarily taking on the melodious lilt of science fiction jargon. In conventional IVF, he went on, the egg and sperm were left together to fertilise just as they would in nature. But with male infertility they had to give nature a helping hand by isolating one of the sluggish sperm and injecting it straight into the egg. And Johnny and I both sit nodding in unison at this new updated version of the birds and the bees, grateful for any crumbs of hope the medical profession might care to bestow upon us in our hour of need.

'As you've no doubt read, the dramatic drop in male fertility is one of the most precipitous changes in the make-up of the human body history has ever recorded. Oestrogen in the water. Additives. Pesticides. It's all still a matter of speculation. Yet up until only seven years ago male infertility was considered untreatable. Sperm donation would have been your only option. But ICSI has changed all that. I'm pleased to say that we are now well placed to help couples in your situation. These days ICSI accounts for a third of all fertility treatments. And our results are very cheering. Very cheering indeed.'

I nod, impressed, secreting this last phrase away for later scrutiny, already cherishing its shiny optimism.

Beside me, Johnny clears his throat, and asks tentatively exactly what our chances of success might be.

'For a couple in your situation . . . probably in the region of . . . one in five,' the doctor says, measuring the words in careful spoonfuls. And even as it falls from his lips, the figure has an instant talismanic ring.

So one in five were saved. Yet that meant eighty per cent would fail. Which sounded terrible, my spirits instantly flagging. I switch back to the one in five. Like a trick of the light. Or the glass that was half empty or half full according to your frame of mind.

'The woman's age is of course the single key factor.' He slides a chart across the table on which the graph line appears to plummet vertiginously from the age of thirty-five. At forty it flattens out, all but extinguished.

I study the flat end of the line, the years seeming to cluster behind me, pushing and jostling me ever nearer to this barren plateau. Youth had seemed a perpetual summer. Despite everything I had read about not leaving it too late, how mysteriously and inexorably time had melted away. I see I've only been half attending as fertility slipped from me, the remainder of my thirties a mere butter-greased slide to the end of hope.

'Let me know when you've had a chance to mull

things over,' Dr Grisham had at last concluded, shaking our hands without warmth. And here we both are, stepping out into the street, a little dazed and shaky. A small child passes us, hand in hand with her mother, a touchingly diminutive figure amongst the crowds that throng the pavement. Beside us, leaning at the wheel of his car, a father of about Johnny's age stops momentarily at the lights, his two sons lolling in school uniform on the back seat. It is as if, though we once walked amongst this great mass of humanity, our path was quietly diverging. I take Johnny's arm, the cacophony of the city a distant commotion, and we walk for a while without speaking.

'So what do you think then?' he says at length, frowning at the ground.

'That we should seize this opportunity with both hands.'

'But there are no guarantees. He was very clear about that.'

'One in five isn't so bad . . .'

He tightens his grip on my hand. 'But the treatment seems to revolve entirely around poking and prodding you. All I have to do is turn up at the end and jerk off into a jam jar.'

'Oh, don't worry about me. I can take it.'

He smiles uncertainly, scanning my face. 'It's your call, Rosie. I don't know what else to say.'

'I told you. I think we should beg, steal or borrow. Hawk the family silver. Do whatever it takes. We'll never forgive ourselves if we don't give this our best shot.'

The tightness in his shoulders seems to drop away, the

stiff set of his face breaking at last into a broad smile of relief, and he nods several times with an awkward jerky motion, as if trying to dislodge all lingering doubt.

I call Tamsin from the cab on the way to the studio, but she's left her answer machine on, so I leave a jaunty update. There was no need for melodrama after all. It had been a shock to find ourselves here; but with any luck it would all be sorted very quickly now. A brief detour. Thank God for medical advances. Intracytoplasmic sperm injection. A small rush of hope lifts me. Perhaps it was only fitting that in the year of the new millennium we should find ourselves rescued by state-of-the-art science, its buoyant wings bearing us forward.

Eight grave faces gaze up from the contact sheet, a dull formality to their clothes and background. Only the chairwoman's portrait gives me a quiet pleasure. A charmless woman, anxious to return to the trading floor as quickly as possible and rudely impatient of my instructions, there is something of her character slyly captured here. But it's a small satisfaction. I select a few frames, circling them without enthusiasm, before pushing them dispiritedly to one side.

In search of a distraction, I log on and find two more e-mails of refusal waiting for me. One from Lucien Freud's gallery. Another from Madonna's publicist. I print them up and put them in the file marked 'Icons and Heroes'. The number of nos was growing at a dispiriting rate. Try again. Fail again. Fail better. I pick up the phone.

'Stephen Hawking? No. Mr Hawking has a blanket policy of not doing any pictures or interviews.'

'Could I send a formal request just in case?'

'There really would be no point.'

'Even if a percentage of the book's profits is being donated to a well-known children's charity?'

'Even if a percentage of profits is being donated to a well-known children's charity.'

'That's it then?'

'That's it, I'm afraid.'

So I turn back to the computer, and punch 'ICSI' into the search engine, hoping to lift my flagging spirits by reading about this miraculous fertility treatment we have now signed on for. I wait while the page resolves itself.

Controversy over fertility wonder technique.

I scan quickly on, my eye snagging in alarm on random headlines:

Injecting a sperm directly into an egg may result in a mentally impaired child.

Hastening on, still hunting fruitlessly for something more reassuring:

Grave genetic concerns over new IVF 'breakthrough'.

It's not too late, I think in panic. *Close the page down. Just pretend you never saw it.* Though already fear is forcing my eye greedily upon the small print. The reports say that despite the fact ICSI now accounted for nearly a third of all IVF treatment, the eldest children conceived by it were still only seven, and little was known about its long-term consequences. Some studies had found that these children had a greater chance of suffering delayed mental development by their first birthday. And a number of specialists had raised serious questions over the potential long-term damage of overriding the natural process of selection, while others expressed concern about the repercussions of the physical disruption when the needle punctured the egg.

Of course, of course. I sit back in my chair. All week in my heart of hearts, I had wrestled with secret uncertainty. *What good could ever come from meddling with nature?*

Within days, the box containing the hormones for the treatment is delivered. The specialist courier company have called to report on its progress throughout the day and by the time it arrives, their assiduous care, together with the four-figure sum we have paid, combine to give the small brown package an alarming potency. Unable to face opening it yet, I place it carefully in the bathroom – away in the farthest, darkest corner – shutting the door quickly.

*   *   *

An explosion in my chest, and I burst upwards out of sleep. Johnny is leaning over me. I have a confused impression I may have been shouting. Though he appears to be speaking, I can make no sense of what it is he is saying. I'm tangled in the marshy sheets and twisted pillows, a mutant creature receding into the darkness of the night, its disturbing musky scent still choking the air.

'It's okay,' he seems to be saying. 'Just a bad dream, babe.'

The hammering of heart easing a little, I reach out and touch the warm flesh of his chest, beginning to separate the contours of the waking world from the nightmare.

'You're all right. You're all right.'

Close against him, the earthly scents are reassuring, the velvet down of skin drawing me back from the hinterlands.

'Don't leave me,' I say in a small voice.

He lies down again, pulling me to him. 'Darling, I'm not planning on going anywhere.'

But already he's tumbling backwards into sleep, and I huddle close until I hear from the slow exhalation of breath that he has slipped away again. Then I remember the box in the bathroom. The little chemistry kit whose potions might conjure up a Frankenstein.

Get a grip, I think, rallying. A clear head was all that was required. Think it through, lay it to rest. I summon up the Defence, who rises stumbling in the dark of the night, straightening a hastily donned wig. *After all, it's*

*hardly as if nature left to her own devices guarantees
infallible results*, he declares in a reassuringly authorita-
tive manner. *What about all those naturally conceived
babies born with birth defects; with Down's syndrome, or
autism, with cleft palates and harelips?*

But before I can prevent it, an indignant Prosecution
is already on her feet, imperiously shouting him down.
*But these were children conceived in good faith. An
entirely different matter from* knowingly *embarking on a
treatment over which there are grave medical question
marks, wouldn't you say?*

And now the dread is at large, chattering and
clattering in the blind void around the bed. Was I really
seeking life at any cost?

I get up, feeling my way through the darkness to the
box in the bathroom and, carrying it carefully, put it
out on the balcony. I can't be sure something toxic isn't
leaking from it, like an odourless poison gas.

Then I remember a photograph of a baby conceived
by this new method of IVF. It had accompanied a
magazine story I read before I had any idea we too would
soon be seeking to walk this path. I search the flat until I
find it. But the face offers no clues. Though I scan its
features carefully for secrets, it appears to be a regular
baby face. No visible deformities of any kind. Nothing to
betray the distorting hand of science. Though it was hard
to know why it should when the reports had been about
hidden developmental problems. The dawn chorus is
twittering now, light spreading faintly beyond the roof-
tops. Suspended in that weightless limbo where night

gives way to day, neither yet quite one thing nor the other, I sit with the scattered magazines all around, gazing and gazing at the little face.

It is as if fear is a genie that has leapt gleefully from its bottle. Should never have read those Internet reports. If I could only erase them from my mind, if I could only get the genie back in the bottle, we'd be on track again. I was meant to begin the treatment tomorrow. Dr Grisham had worked out my cycle and given me clear instructions. But it seemed impossible now. I needed time. Time to work it all out. Yet time is the one thing I don't have. Time is the enemy, sweeping me on to the barren years when there would no longer be choice.

I begin clearing the plates from last night's supper, working carefully in order not to wake Johnny. If he saw me now, it would only trigger fruitless self-reproach. He'd almost certainly try to insist we abandon the treatment. It was my job to protect him. Not to bring further woe to his door. A waft of spicy takeaway, the clouded glasses with their quick scent of wine. In the early morning stillness the clink of cutlery has a harsh precision. And I remember that amongst the clinic's literature there was mention of a counsellor. I'd put the notion aside, assuming it to be mere window-dressing on their part. I had imagined a bored medical student, on some kind of worthy secondment. Someone who would glance surreptitiously at her watch, thinking how much more life had to offer beyond the base urge to procreate. I could hardly blame them. Not so long since I would have agreed. But where else could I turn now success and failure had come to seem such equally untenable prospects?

'We're incredibly lucky, Johnny and I. I know that. We've got a great life together.'

The counsellor nods.

'I mean, it's not that we're desperate or anything like that.'

She nods again, smiling sympathetically.

'Of course, kids would be nice and everything, but . . . We're not like those sad couples you read about. You know, who've got nothing else in their lives . . .'

There is a pause, before she shakes her head, smiling quizically. 'Forgive me, but I'm struggling to see where someone like me might fit into this perfect life of yours?'

I think of all the patients who will take my seat when I'm finished. People who had unsuccessfully undergone a number of treatments and must decide whether to continue. Women who had at last achieved the precious pregnancy, only to miscarry. Couples whose relationships were fragmenting under the pressure of their infertility. Even in this corporate setting, with its synthetic carpet, fluorescent lighting and laminated mock wood furniture, it was as if their troubles whispered and rustled on the dry air. The sensation felt oddly companionable. And despite my doubts, this woman was clearly shrewd and compassionate. The very fact of her employment, with the half-emptied box of tissues on the coffee table, confirmed that fear and anxiety could be part of the process. So I tell her about the reports I have read and confess how unqualified I feel to make the decision now before me.

'Have you thought about contacting Anthony Ling, the clinic's senior embryologist, to talk your worries through with him? After all, he more than anyone must have given the health and ethical issues much thought.'

The suggestion is so startling, I realise I've been imagining a vast white factory in which masked scientists bent absorbed over their test tubes. The role of an embryologist had never crossed my mind. Yet now I thought about it, it was perfectly obvious. The doctor managed the patient and their medication. But the sharp end – the actual business of fertilisation, the sperm's injection into the egg – was done under his or her dexterous hands. It was as if one of the anonymous scientists pulled away their mask, and stepped forward with hand outstretched to greet me.

'Anthony's been a great pioneer in the field. He studied the technique in Brussels ten years ago and was one of the first embryologists to bring the treatment to this country. Anthony Ling. Call him. He's here most days.' She writes down his name and number and gives it to me. 'As long as you're a patient here, you can come and see me as often as you like,' she says, glancing briskly at her watch and brushing down her skirt.

As we rise in unison, static crackles and pops across the chair cover, the synthetic scent of hot nylon like a sneeze in my nostrils.

A blustery wind carries me along the street before setting me down at the college doors. Everyone I pass looks like a student. Wan youthful figures cluster in groups. On the steps it's hard to find a way through their massed ranks as they stand smoking and conversing.

Wandering hesitantly along the corridor, I pass a lecture hall, and pause to peer in through the glass windows. A man I presumed must be Anthony Ling was standing on the platform, writing an equation on an overhead projector. When he finished he stood reflecting on what he'd written, immersed in some inward calculation, while the absorbed faces of his students glowed dimly in the projector light. He was a large man, perhaps in his mid forties, but when he finally looked up, there was a youthful vigour in his manner, a black lock of hair falling foppishly as he addressed his students again. Though his accent was British, he looked as if he might be of East Asian descent. At his concluding comment a great roll of laughter rumbled through the hall and he bowed his head, acknowledging their amusement before dismissing them like a conductor. Then with a great clatter the room rose as one.

*   *   *

'Of course, you're absolutely right to be concerned,' he says, once we have introduced ourselves and adjourned to the college's café. Carrying overflowing coffee cups, we find seats in the far corner, away from the laughing students. 'In my early days of involvement with ICSI, I too had doubts. In fact I must confess my doubts were initially very grave indeed.' He considers me thoughtfully for a moment. 'It's very much down to the individual skills of the practitioner. An embryologist with a hangover is not going to be performing at their best. Even the vibrations from someone passing thirty or forty metres away can upset results.' He sips the hot drink quickly, and settles himself awkwardly into the narrow space.

It was only as time passed, he says, that his concerns were increasingly allayed as he began to see how quick and lively the resulting babies were. He dismissed the reports that suggested developmental problems, saying the research had been fatally flawed in a number of key ways. 'However, I must be honest and say that some of these children may go on to develop genetic flaws in adult life. It's possible.' He shrugs. 'Only time will tell. But then there is every reason to hope that if there *are* repercussions, we will have developed the science to deal with them by then. Things are moving so rapidly now. You only have to read the papers. There are new developments almost every week.'

I am attending so closely to his words that even now he has paused, I realise I'm still earnestly nodding. He smiles.

'And if this helps at all, I have to say I now approach my work each day with joy. My uncertainty has entirely gone. I think the results so far are truly remarkable.'

As if from nowhere, a longing for a sustaining faith of some kind strikes me a savage blow. How had I got this far in life with no discernible beliefs to guide and sustain me? I was a vessel without ballast. It didn't require much turbulence to reveal it. I sit back in my chair, momentarily overwhelmed.

'Listen, if the decision about whether to proceed is causing you great uncertainty, put the treatment to one side,' he says in a kindly manner. 'Come back to it when you've resolved things in your own mind.'

And now, in the absence of a heavenly court, this earthly creator is waiting for me to speak. I rouse myself.

'But each day I'm getting older . . .'

He smiles compassionately, his voice as gentle as a priest's.

'A few months won't make so much difference.'

I sit for a moment, reflecting.

'Is there any possibility I could come and watch you at work?' I ask, with more urgency than I had intended. He opens his hands, in a generous open-palmed gesture.

'Of course!' he laughs. 'My door is always open.'

As soon as I reach home, I take up the phone to make my final call. Last ditch attempt to kick-start an ill-fated project. The publicist laughs. 'You want to photograph David Beckham? You and half the world's press, right?

I've got to be honest with you, it's highly unlikely. But send me an e-mail and I'll run it past him.'

'But it's a long shot?'

'Well, put it this way. He's got some pretty mega deals on the table.'

'Photographic portraits?'

'I really can't disclose details . . .'

'Don't you think it might amuse him to be in the same line-up as the Dalai Lama?'

'You might be better off calling one of those look-a-like agencies.' She laughs that flinty laugh again. 'Just don't hold your breath,' she says before the phone goes down. 'That's all I'm saying.'

D ressed in a blue theatre gown and hat, Anthony Ling greets me jovially in the clinic's reception. 'Hello, hello. I'm afraid we're a little discombobulated today. But welcome!' I shake his hand shyly. Now I'm here, I'm not at all sure what it is I am hoping to find.

In the changing room, I pull on an identical blue gown and hat and emerge looking as if I am a member of the medical team on my way to surgery. Patients in the waiting area glance up deferentially as I pass, and a little flare of liberation buoys me, as if my costume has miraculously sprung me from their powerless ranks.

The laboratory is tiny; the austerity of its bare surfaces

and noisy clatter of air-conditioning impossible to connect with a place where life might be kindled.

'Here's where the eggs are fertilised.' Anthony Ling rests a hand on a giant microscope. 'And this,' he says, throwing open the door of the incubator with a theatrical flourish. 'This is where the developing embryos are stored.' He takes out a Petri dish, and places it gently beneath the microscope, gesturing to me to come closer. 'Three embryos! Two days old. We must be quick though.' He speaks softly, as though mindful of not waking them.

Through the bright white sphere of the eyepiece drift three clusters of swollen cells, like planets adrift in an empty universe. I blink and blink again. Somewhere someone laughs, and I realise it's my own incredulous exclamation. Smaller than a full stop, here was the little tinder spark of life dividing before my very eyes. The hair rising along my arms. A shudder passing down my spine. I shake my head, unable to take it in, and he laughs, 'You, too – once upon a time . . .'

I take one last took through the microscope. But anxious that some careless gesture might end new life or inadvertently muddle it, I'm careful to keep my hands clasped firmly behind my back. Mr and Mrs Goldbloom unwittingly raising Mr and Mrs Maloney's child because of a moment's inattention.

'There's a woman coming into the theatre next door to have these replaced in half an hour. She's getting changed now.'

I think of her hastily slipping off clothes, easing the

rings from her fingers, her breath coming in nervous footfalls. He glances at the clock, and taking the little dish up, returns it to the incubator with care, like a jeweller securing his *pièce de résistance*.

The cold science of it all only took you so far. What kindled these three embryos into life and sustained them, while others withered away? Like some kind of divine alchemy. How many thousands of lives must this man have sprung into being? All that hatching and burgeoning beneath his fingertips. My eye is drawn to his hands, a crazy thought stirring at how easy it would be to believe that some kind of celestial energy must lie coiled there in the sinew and bone.

'Do you meet many patients?' I ask, thinking of the unseen recipient of the embryos so close at hand in the next room.

'It's a funny thing, you know. If you want you can hide away in here and remain remarkably anonymous. And for my own emotional preservation, just to give me some chance of longevity in this business, I have to confess I try not to meet too many. IVF is a painfully disappointing experience for many couples. I'm all too aware the human cost can be immense.' He pauses, regarding me closely for a moment. 'I mean, I often say to patients – don't invest too much in us, you know. We're only human too!' His laughter is rueful.

Out on the street, the light is already waning, the afternoon slipping quickly away. I have a distinct sensation of lightness now, as if the pavement has acquired a pillowy bounce. I buy ingredients to cook a meal for Johnny and make calls I've been putting off for days now. Travelling between meetings, I catch the first intimations of spring on the air.

At home, amongst the scattered post on the mat, I find a manila envelope with an Office Tibet logo. I have to read the letter twice before I can settle on its content. My request for a portrait sitting has been granted. I have half an hour with the Dalai Lama. They offer a day and a time, and request that I notify them with a central London location as soon as possible. Elated, I call immediately to confirm, then on an afterthought ring the clinic to arrange new dates to finally begin treatment.

'Anything,' I recalled Tsering Tashi saying, 'anything is possible!'

5

The box is open on the bed, its contents scattered between the folds of duvet. I must begin by inhaling from the bottle labelled Buserelin at four-hourly intervals. I check the literature again. Each sniff will accumulatively suppress the pituitary gland, it explains, creating an artificial menopause within two weeks. I pause, swirling the liquid to and fro. Then quickly, before my nerve fails me again, I block one nostril and inhale deeply.

As a teenager I'd sometimes experimented with amyl nitrate from a virtually identical bottle. One deep inhalation, and my heart would thunder huge against my ribcage, while a band of iron clenched tight about my head. Later in my twenties, there'd been the occasional snort of cocaine, triggering an elated rush of nervy energy, and an agitated compulsion to share what appeared to be pressingly insightful and witty observations on the world. Though hindsight almost always revealed them to have been nothing of the kind. Later I had learned to avoid the coke heads who bore down on you at parties, trapping you in one of these pointless monologues. Now, however, though I sit braced and waiting, I feel no discernible effects of any kind. Only the faintest acrid taste marks the moment. And after all these anxious weeks, it seems oddly anti-climactic.

As the days pass, I step before the mirror each morning expecting to see the face of an old woman rise up to greet me. Shutting the reproductive organs down enabled them to take control of your body, the doctor has explained. Later they would kick-start it into life again, using new potions designed this time to stimulate eggs in abundance.

The literature warned of possible side effects. Headaches, tiredness, severe hot flushes. Yet as each day ends without any sign of them, I am feather-light with the relief of being finally on our way. My optimism is catching. Johnny sings loudly now, as he takes his morning shower, and is positively jaunty as he scoops up his coat and bag. We bid each other farewell with a playful flirtatiousness, like doting newly-weds in a sitcom, as if we are playing the rituals of marriage like a game.

Two weeks of inhaling four times a day, and finally the dead-eyed doctor announces impassively that the Buserelin has done its work. My reproductive system has been suspended in the frozen winter of a chemically induced menopause. Once a day, I must now inject something from my box of tricks called Gonal F, a hormone designed to stimulate the ovaries to produce eggs in abundance. I can come to the clinic for the injections, or do them myself at home. Most patients, he assured me, were surprised how easily they overcame their initial aversion to the needle.

'Or you could always get your husband to do it,' the nurse says cosily, setting the injection kit out before me. 'I've had lots of women tell me it gets the husband more involved. You know. Brings them closer together.'

She bustles back and forth, showing me how to prepare the potions and fill the syringe. I try to imagine Johnny stabbing with noble resolve at the soft flesh of my leg and privately doubt this. It would only distress him. Far easier to do it myself. Forcing my attention away, I press the button and with an almost imperceptible click, the needle embeds itself in the subcutaneous fat of my leg. The sensation is glancing, infinitesimal. I open the casing again and throw the spent syringe into the special disposal bin. Another spit in the eye of fear, I think triumphantly, observing the tiny jewel of blood that marks the spot. And when I wipe it away, there is nothing, no visible injury of any kind.

At night I often lie awake, pondering on the Dalai Lama's portrait. Initially I had planned a classically formal portrait. But increasingly I see that there is little to be gained by playing this safe – that if this flare from obscurity doesn't burn brightly, it risks being squandered. And hard on the heels of this realisation comes the image of a swarm of butterflies flitting about the Lama's head. Though I instantly dismiss the notion as too saccharine, later, having drifted into an unsettled sleep, I wake again with a start.

What if it were a swarm of insects? Indeed what if it were a strange and beautiful assortment of *creatures* that clustered about him, forming a surreal and rather striking frame? It would be easy enough to gather the images and marry them on the computer once I had his photograph. The flush of inspiration makes my return to sleep an effortless free fall this time, my dreams humming with the agitated rustling and snuffling of living things.

Though I'm careful to do the injections at the designated time every evening, I seldom give much thought to the treatment now. An iconographic image of astonishing beauty holds me spellbound. I spend hours sourcing shapes that will work when cunningly interwoven. Pig-tailed monkeys, anacondas and iguanas. Peruvian giant centipedes, wolf spiders and spiny anteaters. Nature's rich panoply entwined like a garland about the enigmatically smiling face of the Dalai Lama. And very quickly I realise the fever has clamped me in its limpet grip again, the world falling away, tunnel vision closing in. I remember a prestigious portrait prize I've always wanted to enter. Even if the book doesn't work out in the end, a picture like this could open doors. I imagine it published in discerning collections as one of the defining images of the new millennium.

So here I am. Lightly poised to step at last from the shadows.

*   *   *

With my eyes closed, even the smallest sounds seem magnified in the hushed room.

'. . . tension melting away now. Your head filled with radiant light. A warm sustaining light.'

New thoughts to add to the list of things to be organised for the Dalai Lama keep tumbling jauntily into the radiant light. No sooner have I ejected one, than another springs up in its place.

'And in your imagination you have returned to a time and place that was particularly happy for you. A time you have treasured. And you are remembering and reliving it . . .'

I force the thoughts into abeyance. Instead in saturated colour, like switching on a grainy home movie, I resurrect the sun setting over a ruined temple beside a lake in Pham Ngu Lao, while Johnny sits close beside me swigging from a bottle of rum. Bats are dipping low over the water, and fishing boats head home through a silvery dusk that is bringing to a close a day of unparalleled perfection, like a curtain falling softly across a stage.

'Just let your breath come and go. Come and go . . .'

I lie quietly, distractions at last falling away, weightlessness washing in.

'And perhaps you can tell me what mental image you have of your womb?' the counsellor asks quietly. My eyes snap open again.

My womb?

A schoolgirl snicker leaps unbidden in my throat. For some reason the word seems to resonate with earnest feminist baggage. Did other women really carry a picture in their head? Why had no friend ever thought to mention it? Whatever happens, it is inappropriate to laugh, I instruct myself sternly. When the counsellor invited me to be one of the first to join a study she was pioneering into the effects of positive visualisation, I had readily agreed in the sincere hope of improving our chances of success. But though I attempt to summon an image, nothing comes, the bubbles of laughter only fizzing irrepressibly higher. Perhaps this was all a set-up. Some elaborate practical joke. I imagine the door suddenly giving way against Tamsin's collapsing weight as an explosion of laughter jack-knifes her into the room. 'My womb, my womb!' she declaims in a satirically ardent voice, one hand clasped dramatically to her forehead.

Dimly I recall a picture from a biology textbook. But the image is entirely clinical. And all the while the counsellor waits expectantly for my reply. *Christ.* My mental map is apparently androgynous. And then it comes to me. Framed at last in words, the urge to laugh vanishing as if I have been doused in ice-cold water. All these years. All these years, I've clearly just been masquerading as female. Not the least understanding, when actually pressed, of what it really meant. Once again, I'm forced to consider my manifest shortcomings. First, no guiding spiritual framework. Now, no discernible sense of gender.

With new gravity, I strain to imagine this mysterious female organ. Surely it wasn't too late to be inducted into this secret sorority. To rid myself of this telling blind spot before it sabotaged everything that lay ahead.

'Well, I suppose, it's pink and translucent . . .' I begin striking out tentatively. 'And filled with tiny arteries of red. Like the branches of a tree.'

'Okay. And how would you like to visualise the embryo?'

'I imagine . . .' I take a deep breath. How would it be? I close my eyes again and force myself to see something. Anything, the silence demanding words. 'I suppose I imagine a vibrating cluster of cells.'

'Okay. Good. Let's focus now on that image.'

I frown in fierce concentration.

'Your womb pink and translucent, and the foetus a vibrant cluster of cells. And I'd like you to visualise these two elements making a connection.'

Against a Day-Glo pink background, a vibrating grenade twists and turns, bumping in slow motion, like a lurid Gilbert and George canvas.

'So that's the image we'll recall on the day of the embryo transfer. Let's leave it there, shall we? Just lie quietly for a moment. Open your eyes when you're ready.'

Thankfully, the urge to laugh has entirely passed now. I can hear the distant hum of traffic on Great Portland Street, and the bass note of a passing plane, a giddy soporific sensation sinking through me.

At home I find Johnny clearing the spare bedroom, hefting out the debris that has accumulated over the years. He has taken apart the rowing machine, stacked the boxes of VHS tapes, and called a dealer to come and take away his old record collection, lovingly preserved since teenage years.

'I'm on a feng shui bender,' he says, out of breath. 'Time to get organised. Don't want to be caught on the hop.'

The contours of the room have revealed a space more than big enough for a cot. I watch him work for a moment, touched, the months ahead unfurling for a moment, bright with promise. We seem so effortlessly propelled now, life's strands at last meshing with the crisp easeful glide of a zip being zippered.

'Might give it a lick of paint. Pink or blue – what d'you reckon?' he asks, standing back proudly to admire his handiwork, momentarily seeming to forget our unspoken pact not to make any direct reference to what the future might or might not hold.

'White,' I say evasively, taking his hand. 'White would be just fine . . .'

The Dalai Lama shoot is almost upon me now, and close behind it, the final stages of treatment. Every conceivable contingency has been covered, the day carefully streamlined to run at maximum efficiency. I have booked a central London studio, hired the best assistant available, and invested in an esoteric collection of herbal teas. I had decided to abandon the concept of swarming animals, preferring after much indecision to resurrect the original concept of a portrait distinguished by exquisite simplicity. I never tired of people's open incredulity. 'The Dalai Lama!' they'd say, eyes widening in gratifying disbelief. 'Really? How amazing!'

Yet the pleasurable anticipation at the shoot's approach was always coloured by the thought of everything that would come so hard on its heels. The operation to extract the eggs. The uncertainty about whether any would fertilise. Then a second operation to replace the resulting embryos. And after that, the two-week wait until we would know whether I was at last pregnant.

At night I walk the flat room by room, restlessly straightening pictures and plumping cushions. I try to visualise the great man arriving, and settling himself in the chair. The entourage clustering at his side, like courtiers vying for proximity. Seven or eight people, Tsering Tashi had said. A secretary, a religious assistant, three security men, a representative and personal attendants. The Dalai Lama preferred not to be directed too much, Tashi had warned, preferring just to be himself.

'Will he mind smiling?'

'Oh, no!' Tashi had tittered like a schoolboy, seeming to find the question inordinately amusing. 'I think you will find that His Holiness is a most proficient and natural smiler. Of that we can be most certain.'

I wonder whether the Dalai Lama bothered with small talk. Perhaps I should be bold and attempt a stimulating discussion of some kind. Gabriel had maintained a keen proprietorial eye on the whole enterprise, and sent me one of the Dalai Lama's numerous books. This morning I had taken it up and read at random.

There are many people who do not follow any religion. The important thing is that their life should be meaningful, in other words that deep down they should be happy. Happy, but without harming others. If our satisfaction means that others have to suffer, then sooner or later we will too.

A greatly revered man of our times. Fixed by my emulsion, surely it was not unreasonable to hope that his spiritual credibility might anoint me by proxy, propelling me out of professional mediocrity. The rising scent of lilies and tuber rose is like a glancing swoon. But then only a few days later there would be this operation to face. I reach out to adjust the vase, but the lily petals all fall away, leaving ugly bare stamens. All the flowers are dying, I see now, little heads of tuber rose snapping at the tips. It was unfortunate that the portrait and the operation had drifted so close to jostle each other in this way. Hope trampling hard on the heels of trepidation, trepidation trampling hope.

I keep these worries from Johnny – desire to protect him an entirely automatic habit of mind. But without explanation he ceremoniously takes up residence in the kitchen now. Every evening I return home to some new and elaborate dish. One night pan-fried partridge breast, the next Pacific ceviche. We light candles and exchange inconsequential news as we eat, the homemade food serving as an infinitely preferable substitute for any anxious discussion of what might lie ahead.

A ll week the weather is stormy and unsettled. I travel to and from the clinic for frequent monitoring now. Too many eggs and they will have to hastily suspend treatment. Too few and our chances of success dwindle accordingly. Mostly I go alone. Johnny was adamant that he didn't want to tell anyone at work about the treatment. Even in the reasonably enlightened setting of an advertising agency, he feared people assuming that his infertility negated virility. An ability to exchange blokeish joshing and asides with the men, and to flirt lightly with the women, was entirely integral to the social rituals that oiled the working day. He dreaded the whispers at the water cooler, *poor old Johnny shooting blanks*, instantly reducing him, if only in his own mind, to an emasculated object of compassion. And mostly I'm happy to go on my own. To do what we can to keep the disruption to a minimum. Not to get obsessed with it all. Not to fall into that fatal trap of letting the whole business derail our lives.

At the last visit Dr Grisham had pointed out the dark areas on the ultrasound that indicated the developing eggs, and estimated there to be about twelve or so. 'You're responding nicely,' he had said dispassionately.

Despite the indignity of my semi-naked state and the unpleasantness of the cold probe lodged inside me, pride and relief had flared briefly. Another hurdle cleared. Another furlong nearer. As the treatment draws to its conclusion, an uncomfortable sensation of fullness sometimes comes and goes low across my belly as the dozen follicles swell, each to the size of a one pence piece.

Today, in the overheated consulting room, the doctor observes the ultrasound screen for some time before announcing that the eggs are almost ready for harvesting. I dress hastily while he snaps off his rubber gloves and sits straight-backed at his desk, muttering quick calculations.

'Two days' time, we'll stop the home injections, one late-night injection at the hospital to ripen the eggs. Then . . . return for the egg collection thirty-six hours later.' He scribbles the dates and rips the paper from the pad with a flourish. 'So the Profasi injection at midnight on Tuesday, then we'll need you back here for egg collection, first thing Thursday morning.'

'Thursday!' my voice echoing foolishly. The day of the Dalai Lama shoot. I shake my head. 'I can't. I've got a portrait sitting . . . It'll have to be either the day before, or the day after — ' The note remains quivering in mid air, his hand immobilised. 'I've got a commitment I can't possibly change, you see.'

He returns the note to his desk, and clears his throat. 'A day earlier or later will almost certainly scupper us,' he says implacably. 'Timing is all I'm afraid.'

I sit down, thinking quickly. Though there is no way I can possibly reschedule the Dalai Lama, I *could* just call this round of treatment off and start all over again in a month or two. Grisham rests his dead eyes on me, while behind him the nurse tidies the trolley with feigned absorption. Everything has stilled in the over-heated room. After a moment or two, he loosens his tie and dabs irritably at his damp upper lip.

And then inspiration comes. 'What if we make the egg collection very early that morning? I could go straight on to my appointment.'

His expression is incredulous. 'You'll have been sedated. Frankly, you won't be up to anything more than being taken straight home and put to bed.'

The scales waver before me. Can hardly believe we've come so far, only to have to abandon the treatment so late.

'Only you can decide what your priorities are . . .' he says, attempting a tolerant smile.

He's probably thinking of the clinic's league tables, I think. Blown off course by a tunnel-visioned career woman. Behind him the nurse hovers at the trolley, her hands going through the motions of activity while she waits enthralled for my answer. Anyone could see that she was a proper woman, a womanly woman, scented like vanilla, with bosoms soft as pillows. The kind whose maternal commitments would always come first, while here I sat all witch-like and warty. *Prospective motherhood or career. Career or prospective motherhood.* The scales teeter.

The consultant's tolerant smile is stiffening. I think of the Dalai Lama's portrait, without which I have come to see I am doomed to loiter forever in obscurity. Of the rarity of the good fortune that has brought the opportunity to my door.

'I think . . .' I say, playing for time, knowing how shocked he's going to be when I cancel. 'I'm afraid . . .'

'It would be a great shame when things have gone so well, not to give this your best shot. Do you not think?'

The scales shift again with a queasy see-saw motion. All those hormones and injections. And even now this belly full of eggs. Any one of them with the potential to become our child. The child that has eluded us for so long now.

'Of course,' I say, sick at heart even as I concede it. 'Thursday. Thursday it is then.'

And as I head for the door, navigating more from memory than sight, the Dalai Lama's image is melting before me, curling in on itself, like a frame of celluloid caught too long in the projector's heat. Before my hand has even found the door, the edges of the frame have already blackened and evaporated all around him. The last thing to fade is his mouth, the ironic smile lingering even after the rest has powdered to dust.

Out on the street, the air is expectant and stretched. Passers-by instinctively hasten their step, unsettled by the pressure in the atmosphere as it quickens and teeters. When the thunder finally sounds, its mighty echo ricochets along the city skyline and within moments the smell of fumes is swept away by the sharp metallic scent of rain. The first drops are as warm as tears, splashing in my hair and across my cheeks.

6

That night, Johnny had been so sympathetic, that despite my resolve to be as matter-of-fact as possible, I hadn't been able to prevent a self-pitying tear or two from falling. He said that though it had been a painful decision, he thought it the right one. And that my success in securing someone of the Dalai Lama's stature only showed what could be achieved when one set one's mind to it. We were eating chicken and white wine stew with gremolata, and even though the kitchen was now filled with teetering piles of dirty dishes, the stew's soupy juices and his cheering words were beginning to take effect.

'Darling, it's his loss in the end. There are plenty of other fish in the sea.' He had been about to fill my glass with wine before remembering it was currently under embargo and, as he plucked back the bottle, I felt a sudden surge of resentment at the patent untruth of his words.

'No one ever said this was going to be easy,' he'd said consolingly, as we lay in bed that night. And though I said nothing, I had gone to sleep with an unsettled feeling of grievance, almost as if an apology might have been in order.

*   *   *

Morning brought little respite. All those questions I could have asked the doctor, if I hadn't been so distracted by the final demise of the book. 'Will it hurt?' I might have said. 'Should I be this scared?' But even if I had, those dead eyes would only have gazed uncomprehendingly back at me. Something flittered uneasily. An unravelling. The yearning for certainty returning. Only the thought of Anthony Ling at work soothes me, softening the cold science of it all. The deftness of those confident hands; the quick darting motion puncturing the egg, connecting tissue, triggering life.

The clinic tell me he has taken a few days off to finish a research paper. Though he will be back in time to oversee the fertilisation of our eggs, he will not be available for consultation before then. They give me the number of the colleague who is covering for him. But on the whim of a moment I call his mobile, and though he sounds distracted, he sounds convinced enough by my proposal. 'A photographic essay on hands? What a splendid notion! I'd be most honoured.' He would be working from home all week, he says, but would be more than happy to spare me half an hour, and we agree a time the following afternoon.

Though it was true the suggestion had come to me on the spur of the moment, some time ago I genuinely had begun a collection of photographs on hands, hoping it might become a book. I still had them somewhere, with the working title *Creative Hands* scrawled on the folder's spine. I'd begun by photographing a healer's hands.

Then a pianist, a midwife and a gardener. My favourite had been the lithograph I made of a sculptor's hands; the strong fingers ingrained with plaster in the pores, and welts where the mallet chafed the thumb and forefinger. I should resurrect the project, I think. It had been a good idea. I could look them all out, dust them down.

Anthony Ling opens his front door and stands for a moment shading his eyes against the dazzle of sunlight. He has been up most of the night working to complete his paper, he explains as he helps carry my equipment into his study. 'You'll have to forgive the disorder.' There are papers and coffee cups strewn across the desk. As I stack my bags, I see the room also houses a vast collection of fossils clustered densely along the mantelpiece and book-shelves, and pause to take them in, astonished at the sheer quantity. Anthony steps forward, chuckling.

'Aha. Yes. Behold a boyhood passion that has never abated. Trilobites, eurypterids, dinosaur eggs . . .' He is instantly animated, a childlike enthusiasm casting off exhaustion. 'This one was found in a neolithic cave site. This from an Egyptian tomb.' He holds them up in turn, caressing them. 'Have you ever seen a crinoid?' He turns it to catch the light. 'Double blossom stems and look – look here. A perfect imprint of the feeding cilia.'

I nod admiringly, catching his excitement.

'Early Jurassic. One hundred and fifty million years old.' He picks up another piece of rock with the dainty imprint of a dancing fish. 'Something pleasingly chasten-ing about the great sweep of evolution they record, don't you think? How very tiny we humans are within it.'

Close by I hear the sudden shouts of children, their feet stampeding past the study door. Expecting them to burst in, I turn quickly but Anthony Ling remains lost in thought, his eyes upon the collection, a reflective smile hovering at his lips. Somewhere a distant door slams and the voices fade from earshot.

'Your children?'

He nods absently. Of course he had children. The house was probably teeming with them. I imagined them clambering and swarming, while he sat amongst them, smiling beatifically. I wonder whether he'd be offended if I ask more. Too many questions surely breaching the etiquette between doctor and patient. But I'm enjoying it here, something compelling about the off-stage hints of another life. He rubs his eyes, yawning, and I hastily take up the Hasselblad.

'To work then.'

I pull up a chair for him, and we talk a little about his work as I set the camera up. His paper was on cloning, he says, and he fully expected it to stir up further controversy. It was a subject that tended to incite a great deal of fear and misunderstanding. Then he yawns more widely still. After a moment or two we lapse into silence, and he sits quietly with his hands folded in his lap, the late afternoon light falling across them. He appears so deep in thought he might almost be at prayer, and I work as quietly as I can, framing them carefully, observing how neatly the fingers dovetail and how white his nails appear against the dark skin. He adjusts his hands fractionally, and I glimpse the crinoid still cupped in his palm. It almost resembles a small foetus curled there, and a joy rises in me, the little fossil lending an accidental resonance I could never have invented.

'Okay. Sorry about all this fiddling. But I think . . . I think we're finally there.'

He makes no response, only the soft rasp of his breath in the quietness of the room. I take my eye from the camera and see he has fallen asleep, his head to one side, the gentle smile slid clean away. Somehow, it doesn't feel right to continue now. I stand uneasily for a moment, the windows like judgemental eyes at my back, pricking me into self-consciousness. I feel like a thief, hovering covetously.

I bend uncertainly to the eyepiece again. Before me the image I have come to collect. His interlocked fingers remain perfectly still, but already the light is fading, the contrast between the highlights and shadows blurring, the little fossil beginning to be swallowed by darkness. My finger hovers impatiently at the trigger. Then quickly, clumsily, I take the picture, the clunk of the shutter breaking the silence. Then another one, just in case. Anthony Ling jolts into wakefulness for a moment, before his heavy lids slowly close again and the gentle rattle in his throat resumes. I can't bring myself to continue. It feels undeniably like stealing. I begin packing everything away again, working as quietly as I can.

Stepping into the corridor, I almost collide with a woman struggling with bags of shopping.

'Whoopsy!' she swings her weight casually to skirt me, apparently unsurprised to find a stranger stepping unexpectedly from the study.

'You can see yourself out, can you?' she calls over one shoulder, hurrying on her way down the dark corridor.

'Yes, that's fine.' I stop, craning my head after her, hoping to catch a better glimpse, realising this must be his wife.

'He's asleep,' I inform her departing back. 'Thought I'd better just creep away and leave him in peace.'

She pauses at the foot of the stairs and rests the weight of the bags for a moment. 'No doubt soon as he wakes, he'll be up and off again. All those babies to make.' And laughing sardonically, she sets off up the stairs, huffing and puffing at each step.

A series of abstract watercolours hang in the hall. The signature on them might even be Anthony's, it's hard to be sure. I open the front door reluctantly.

'Bye then,' I call. But she's already out of earshot. 'And thanks . . .' I add to no one in particular.

I pin the print on the studio board. And at times a fleeting glance might catch a quiet poetry in its stillness. But even moments later I can look again and find the enchantment gone, no more than a pair of hands after all. I cut out the tiny version from the contact sheet and store it like a four-leaf clover in my wallet.

*   *   *

Midnight in the quiet hospital, the corridors and lifts all empty now, most patients abandoned to sleep. Johnny and I follow the signs, walking side by side, speaking in soft respectful undertones. Somewhere I once read that a peak in deaths and emergencies comes in the small hours of the morning as the circadian cycle dips low. But for now the nurses sit quietly, pools of light illuminating their paperwork as they stoop their heads, absorbed.

I'm seen immediately by a nurse, and the injection in the muscle of my thigh is quick and virtually painless. The cluster of twelve eggs growing inside me will apparently now be triggered to ripen by this new hormone, ready for harvesting the day after tomorrow. I'm like a great chicken about to lay, I think, faintly repulsed, walking the length of the corridor with care now; the grotesque and the absurd strangely entwined in this dance with science.

While Johnny goes to collect the car, I lean against the columns of the hospital exit, staring blindly into the soupy night sky. A man half hidden by bundles of flowers and a bottle of champagne struggles for a moment with the glass door. I hasten to hold it for him, and he steps out into the dark street.

'Cheers!'

I'm about to turn away but something in his face snags my eye. He smiles briefly, then double takes too, his mouth falling open in astonishment.

'Rose!'

'Nick! My God . . .'

We stand mutually astonished.

'Rose Nichols,' he says, his voice catching, and we gaze at one another smiling foolishly, such a complex weight of memory opening between us, we are at a loss how to proceed.

'What on earth brings you here at this godforsaken hour?' I manage, rescuing us both, and he rallies, gathering himself.

'Baby . . . My wife's just had another baby. This afternoon. We had a little boy.' He holds up the tumbling bouquets, beaming. 'We've been deluged, so I'm taking some home. Going to check on his little sisters and crash . . . I tell you, never mind poor Bella, I'm absolutely knackered.'

Age has bestowed blandness, the once dashing features coarsened by middle age. The memory of speeding along a deserted road at midnight comes to me, both of us whooping as the dial swung past a hundred. Of looking on in horror as he was head-butted in a drunken brawl one Christmas, with tinsel winking all about him as he fell, spattering blood like holly berries. Before me the impetuous youth of old now appears to have become a disconcertingly convincing embodiment of establishment man. Settled man. Wife and three children man. Once he had sparked a bittersweet romantic yearning in me. We had circled one another warily, some mysterious forbearance keeping us teetering tantalisingly on the cusp, before different universities had swept us off on diverging paths. A wistful thought escapes before I can suppress it. How different life might be now, if I had pushed for resolution all those years ago.

'Congratulations!' I say, hastily recalling myself.

'What about you? Husband? Kids?' he gestures towards me, as if through the myopia of happiness.

'Me? Oh well . . . married, but no kids.'

'That figures – you were never exactly the maternal type, were you?'

My attempt at laughter gutters in my throat. 'Too busy trying to change the world.'

'I remember. Same old Rose then . . .'

'Same old Rose.'

He laughs, entertained by this Peter Pan notion, and for a brief moment I am this arrested adolescent, snapping gum with an insouciant swagger. Then my spirits abruptly sag, all the fight going out of me. It occurs to me he's probably about to ask what brings me to this hospital at midnight, and too tired to perpetuate the lie, much less to share the truth, I step back quickly, anxious to get away. A feral furtiveness. The shifting weight of eggs. Then the hoot of the car, and Johnny leaning forward at the wheel to urgently beckon me on.

'Give that baby a kiss from me, will you . . .' I raise a hand in farewell, setting off with my strange cargo.

Somewhere in the far distant world, polar ice caps are melting, and ethnic wars devastating communities. But as we journey to the clinic through early morning traffic together, we are the centre of our universe, the axis on which everything else is contingent. Wanting to avoid compassionate scrutiny, we have said nothing to friends, and simply dropped quietly out of the working week. Last night, I had toyed with roast turbot in a spicy lime and coconut marinade, and neither Johnny or I had exchanged a single word about what the morning might hold.

Every now and then, as the car speeds us on our way, I discreetly attempt to read Johnny's pensive profile. For while my eggs are collected in the operating theatre, he must simultaneously produce a sperm sample. And it was only upon waking with a start in the early hours of this morning, it had occurred to me that if under the pressure of expectation he fails, everything so far will have been for nothing. And in the hope of preventing this very thought occurring to him too, with all its attendant power to become a self-fulfilling prophecy, I have kept up a relentless flow of inconsequential conversation. But I could see he was only half attending, his responses distracted and desultory. I reach out and touch his arm gently.

'What are you thinking?'

To my relief, he shakes his head and laughs.

'I was thinking about all those records I gave away. How it would have broken my teenage heart to know I might do that one day.'

Consigned for so long to the sidelines, I realise he is at last taking his place beside me and the realisation touches me deeply. I lean forward, grazing the morning softness of his newly shaved cheek with my lips. Then we draw up outside the clinic's discreet facade, and fear – as if from nowhere – fleets through me like the flick of a whip.

Why was it that the whole process felt so fundamentally unsettling? After all, every week brought stories of far newer and more bizarre IVF breakthroughs. And yet of course, strictly speaking, it *was* unnatural. Not just because it used science to artificially duplicate the moment of conception. It was more than that. It felt in some fundamental way, a transgression. Providence had failed to bless us, and instead of accepting our fate with quiet sadness and dignity as we would have had to in the old days, we mutinously attempted to thwart the hand we had been dealt with vast sums of money and medical expertise.

In the reception area, a nurse gives us each a form to sign, smiling cheerily at our waxen faces. 'If you could just sign these, Mr Mitchell can go off to do his sample, and you can pop into a gown so you'll be nice and ready for theatre.'

I cast a cursory glance at the form. A series of questions on how the embryos might be used, and how they might be stored. It asks for consent to use my eggs in my own treatment and I tick the relevant boxes without hesitation. But then it goes on to ask for consent to use my eggs and embryos in treating other infertile couples, and to elect how long I would wish to store any superfluous embryos.

I hadn't anticipated this. Hadn't begun to consider

what larger issues might lie beyond the morning's egg collection. Suddenly it seemed that life, having so long proved elusive, now threatened to burst the confines of the body and spring like untended seeds all about us. Of course the cluster of cells and secretions about to be taken from both of us needed to be looked after if successfully united. Twelve eggs offered the possibility of twelve lives. And since only a maximum of three could be returned, that left potentially nine remaining embryos in limbo. It was perfectly obvious now I paused to consider it. And tucked up in their vats of liquid nitrogen, who else's responsibility but ours could they possibly be? It was a kind of theoretical parenting. Perhaps the closest to parenting we might ever come.

Beside me, the nurse stands waiting, smiling pleasantly, while I hastily attempt to don the mantle of theoretical mother considering the needs of our theoretical shadow family. And already I find my concern at the prospect of no life is entirely countered by this entirely opposite concern at the prospect of superfluous life and its consequences. For the first time I try to envisage these little embryos suspended in the deep freeze. Would they be tiny babies, *our* tiny babies, bagged up like frozen peas, or merely cell clusters? They were certainly *potential* babies. And as potential babies surely it was our duty to offer them the chance of viability. And in doing so, let a couple who had longed and prayed, just like us, have a chance. Yet one fine day we might turn a corner and find ourselves walking towards a child who looked remarkably like one of us. Always somewhere you might carry this thought; your child passing you by without a second glance. Surely that way madness lay? The panic was rising again, forking through my heart, through my stomach, now the sinewy knot of small intestine. The teetering distress of being asked to be judge and jury on a case whose complexities I only dimly comprehended. Hadn't I once debated this very issue as a student? At what stage did an acorn become an oak? And yet how different the considerations felt now the issue was so pressingly our own. I take a deep breath. They are cell clusters, I tell myself soothingly, as if to a child. Only cell clusters.

(i) Be allowed to perish.
(ii) Treat others.

But still my pen hovers. Then I reach out and slash a fierce proprietorial 'no' to donation and 'yes' to allowing them to perish. The nurse stretches out her hand and I recall her presence with a start. '*Christ*,' I attempt a comical grimace, and thrust the form at her as if it were an examination paper, glad to be rid of it. Then Johnny and I stand up and walk in opposite directions without so much as a backward glance.

The table of the operating theatre is flooded in a harsh light that falls away to darkness at its edges, like a set lit for some kind of noirish movie scene. A scene in which I am disconcertingly sprawled centre stage. More perplexingly still, far from making me drowsy, whatever sedative is shimmering through the drip in my hand, is filling me with the velvet roll of a cat's purr. And though I am lying naked from the waist down, with knees splayed, while Dr Grisham delves in an undignified manner between my legs, I have, in truth, never felt more at one with the world. Kittenish conviviality rising in effervescent arpeggios.

'Can you sing?' I ask the nurse who stands beside me holding my hand, her mouth and nose veiled by a mask.

'Me? Sing? No way.' She laughs a rich arc of merriment at the notion. 'Not a note. She can though . . .' she says nodding at her friend. 'Sings in a church choir she does.'

'For my sins.' The other nurse's eyes crinkle above her mask.

'I sing too,' I cry, delighted. 'I love to sing. Let's all sing an a cappella number shall we?'

There are nervous titters from behind the masks, and somewhere close by, a muffled consultation with the anaesthetist. With amused detachment, I form a dim impression that my levity is causing some concern. Though I can feel occasional twinges as Grisham's tweezers seek out the twelve tiny eggs, the sensation of well-being makes the ache appear far, far away, like someone else's experience entirely. To my right, I glimpse Johnny, a ghostly figure in the gloom. He must have delivered his sample, before slipping in here to join me.

Close by from the shadows, Anthony Ling's voice calls out, keeping count, as Grisham successfully extracts another egg. My joy grows greater still at his proximity.

There he was, waiting to whisk the eggs away and set to work. With everyone clustered close about me, the arc of overhead lights enclosing us against the darkness that lay beyond, it was as if we had set sail on a journey together, our loyal attendants forming this congenial troupe. I attempt the first few bars of a half-remembered song, but the faces all about me work on absorbed. Only Grisham turns briefly, his distracted head swing a magnificently well observed parody of a tetchy professional attempting serious work under trying circumstances.

'What is *in* that stuff?' I ask, laughing with the sheer delight of it all, at the heart-wrenching perfection with which everyone was playing themselves. I crane my head backwards to catch a glimpse of the anaesthetist standing behind me.

'Ahhh, now that would be telling, wouldn't it?' His upside-down face smiles archly at me. 'My secret recipe, you see.' His camp inflection and gleaming teeth, reveal that the author of my liberation from all worldly care appears to bear an astonishing resemblance to a children's party entertainer. Here then was the solution to all life's sorrows. A veinful of his potion and you could travel joyfully, whatever the outward realities. No angst. No yearning. All troubling moral dilemmas vanished, as if in a puff of smoke. What a masterstroke of casting this wizard with his potions was.

It dawns on me that if I am to make a convincing job of my role as patient in this scene, I should show some concern about Dr Grisham's progress.

'How many eggs have you got?' I ask, straining for

gravity, lifting my head to address him as he intently observes the ultrasound screen.

'Twelve. And I—' he was probing carefully, the dull ache flaring distantly '—think that's the last.' He glances over at my dislocated face framed by the v of my legs.

'All twelve!' I sing out, triumphantly beaming upon my solemn attendants. 'This man's a genius!'

The overhead lights cast harsh shadows on his humourless face, the muscles at his mouth twitching a fleeting disdain.

'We've done just fine,' he says impassively.

At home, Johnny helps me climb weakly into bed and volunteers to get a Vietnamese takeaway. I settle luxuriously, flicking through the dross of daytime television, comforted by the unaccustomed indulgence of it all.

'There he is!' Johnny says sharply, on his way to the door, pointing urgently at the screen. I catch a momentary glimpse of a familiar-looking actor in a passionate embrace, but my finger has already pressed the remote control and a daytime talk show now fills the screen. I punch buttons, summoning up a wrestling match, and a cookery demonstration, before finally returning in time to find the end credits now rolling. The name Bill Kelly fleets across the screen.

'That was him! Mr Postcard from Paradise,' he says, amused, heading for the door. 'Disappearing on us again.'

I eat the takeaway in a half drowse, remembering our journey across Vietnam and the carefree couple who played there. There is a serenity about having come this far, the opiate still ebbing pleasantly in my veins. Even the thought of the Dalai Lama cannot jangle me today. I think of Anthony Ling gazing through the microscope. It was up to him now. Our fate, in his hands. The warmth of the bed encloses me, spangled light on the wall brightening and dimming as clouds pass quickly across the sun, until unaccountably buoyed by hope, I am lulled to sleep.

I wake early and dress quickly, yesterday's hilarity on the operating table a bad memory I can't face dealing with just now. The traffic on the way to the studio lurches and halts, tired faces at the wheel, red tail lights flaring belligerently. Several times I almost hit the brake too late, gritting my teeth in anticipation of the crash of metal.

'You will call me, won't you, darling?' Johnny had said, pausing to embrace me, on his way to work. 'The minute you hear anything.'

'Of course.' I had tried to sound offhand.

Anthony Ling had assured me he would ring and update me as soon as he got to the clinic, and more than once I catch myself checking to see that the phone lying beside me is fully charged and switched on. At my studio, I can't find a car-parking space and when I eventually do, it is so narrow I have to park with the car encroaching into the road. But I press the lock and walk away anyway. No point in worrying about the small stuff. Not today.

Climbing the steep stairs, my breath clouds the cold air before me. The scent of the studio as I open the door and the echo of feet on wooden floorboards is familiar and instantly reassuring. Sitting at the dishevelled desk, I clear a space and write a quick letter to Tsering Tashi, reiterating how very sorry I am for having had to cancel at such short notice, and how grateful I would be if he would let me know when the Dalai Lama was next planning a trip to the UK. But I know already, from my lengthy conversation with him, that it would not be for a long time. For a while I gather scattered prints, tidying them into projects. The sharp scent of developer solution, and the shiny slipperiness of the photographic paper, soothes me. But when I try to stack them they skim off one another as if printed on thin cushions of air.

In the dark room I push the trays into parallel lines, select a negative and switch on the enlarger light. This had become my recreational space. These days it served no practical purpose. Screened by two sets of black curtains, it offered a secret world. And usually time was suspended here, images blooming sweetly beneath my fingertips.

But I can't lose myself today, my ear on fire for the call that will tell me if any eggs have successfully fertilised. If any have made it through the night. Bent over the trays, I think of Anthony Ling on his morning rounds. Peering intently through his telescope at the Petri dishes, scrutinising closely for signs of life. Strange round splashes are forming on the photograph as I work, some flaw in the paper bleaching small spots like fairy dust. They spread quickly as I watch with distracted irritation. I wonder for a disoriented moment if I'm hallucinating them.

The shrill ring in the studio's stillness makes me drop the tongs with a clatter. I'm straining to anticipate him from the tone of his greeting alone, nerves drawn tight as violin strings.

'Well,' Anthony Ling says cheerfully, 'we've not done too badly. Three embryos look promising this morning. We'll keep an eye on them, see how they develop over the coming day.'

I thank him quickly, anxious for him to return to his watch. And when I put the phone down I feel strangely deflated. *Was there no end to these hurdles?* I wonder, wearily. You'd no sooner leapt one, than the next was looming forbiddingly before you. Johnny however is jubilant at the news when I call. I can hear that he is smiling from ear to ear.

Through the window, the fluorescent-lit offices on the opposite side of the street draw my eye. Men in white shirts and ties sit at row upon row of desks. I watch their mouths mutely opening and closing, their animated hand gestures. Somewhere across town our potential offspring were – with any luck – busy splitting and dividing in their glass dish. The thought made me light-headed. And all the while Anthony Ling would be bustling to and fro, watching and waiting. Hard to imagine them dividing in that chilly incubator with an autonomy all their own. Easier somehow to think of them drying into papery husks now they were cast adrift from the warm embrace of the human body. A man near the window throws his head back, guffawing, and I watch dispassionately as his back spasms backwards too, teeth bared to the ceiling, eyes squeezed closed by the pressure of gaping mouth. His colleague is pointing to his watch, wagging a teasing finger of admonishment at him, and I come to with a start, remembering I should be somewhere else by now. As I shovel contact sheets into my bag, and hurry down the steep stairs, a tensile vibration resonates through me like a high note through glass.

The gown gapes at the back, chill air along my spine, though I strive modestly to hold it closed as I walk the same walk to the operating table again. Classical music is playing softly and here is the counsellor at my elbow, smiling warmly. The doctor is a different one today. Dead Eye apparently unavoidably detained elsewhere. Heartier and more forthcoming, Dr McKinmont pats my arm in a friendly manner.

'All right my dear? You just relax now . . .'

He has eyebrows that burst exuberantly from beneath his operating hat, and a bustling merriment that makes his stout form appear quick and nimble as he moves about the room. He was the kind of man who enjoyed a nice drop of Claret, I think. And perhaps a Sunday afternoon game of golf, and the occasional evening of light opera. I find I'm grateful for his avuncular manner, relieved to be delivering myself into such cheerful hands. Somewhere in the darkness behind my head, I catch a fleeting glimpse of Johnny. We smile reassuringly at one another. Then the counsellor leans forward.

'Okay? Close your eyes, and I'll take you through the relaxation.'

I do as she says, snapping out the oppressive glare of steel and lights, becoming aware of the wooden rigidity in every muscle.

'They're putting two embryos back. You know that, don't you?' she whispers.

I nod quickly. Don't want to think about the embryos lost along the way. From twelve to three. Now from three to two. Like water slipping through my outstretched fingers.

'Okay. Breathe deeply,' she says. 'Tension melting away now. Your head filled with radiant light. Warm sustaining sunshine. And in your imagination you have returned to a time and place that was particularly happy for you.'

I will the scene before my mind's eye, but today it comes juddering alarmingly, out of focus. After a moment, satisfied at the slowness of my breath, I hear the counsellor whisper to the doctor that he can proceed.

'Prop your legs up for me, would you, my dear?' he says in his jolly voice.

The speculum is cold. I glance briefly across at Johnny. Perhaps the glitter of tears in his eyes is no more than a trick of the light. Yet I am struck anew at what a travesty this was of the private act that brought most of us into this world; the bare operating table, the urgent voice of the counsellor in my ear, my husband an anxious bystander, while a masked medical team bent, intently craning between my legs, the most hidden part of me now the most public. *Nothing could be further removed from intimacy or passion,* I think with sudden loathing. An operation without an illness, a conception that might ultimately yield no life. I close my eyes again, wishing the whole thing over, no bliss-filled sedative to ease my way today.

'Doctor McKinmont is inserting the tube now.' The counsellor's voice again. I strive to keep my breathing regular, and to unclench the muscles that bunch themselves reflexively against the discomfort. 'And I want you to imagine your womb. A pink sphere, filled with red blood vessels.'

The probing sensation makes the image almost impossible to sustain. For the first time I wonder how I am going to get through this.

'And now, the first embryo is being inserted. A vibrant collection of cells, dividing and expanding.'

I will my body still.

'And your womb is enclosing and embracing this vibrant bundle of cells, holding it close . . .'

Hello, hello there! Welcome! Outwardly my eyes may be screwed tightly closed, but inwardly I'm like the distracted hostess of a cocktail party, manfully struggling to maintain the rictus of a social smile. *I'm so very delighted you could join us.*

'And now the second embryo . . .'

'Still as you can, my dear.' The concentration in the doctor's voice spurs me on. I summon the hostess once more, and back she comes, gamely fluffing up her hair, and baring her teeth again. *Come in, take a seat. Do, please, make yourself at hoooooome* . . . A stabbing sensation so fierce, I can't prevent the involuntary spasm that jolts my body.

'Sorry, sorry . . .'

'Not to worry.' Dr McKinmont's jolly voice sounding a little strained. 'Let's have another pop at it, shall we?'

At last he clears his throat and stands back, as the music falls in melancholy conclusion.

'All right, my dear. Well done. That's lovely.' He pats my leg, and I feel the warm modesty of the gown cover me again, returning me to myself.

The nurses leave me lying quietly for half an hour in a side room, while Johnny sits beside me holding my hand, as if in shared post-coital repose. 'No sex for the next two weeks,' Dr McKinmont had instructed us with mock sternness as I was wheeled out of the theatre. 'Chances are it'd be fine. But better to err on the side of caution, hey?' He was pulling off his gloves and gown, apparently in a hurry. I imagined him returning to a comfortable house somewhere in the Home Counties, to an equally cheery and bustling wife stoking the fire, and strapping teenage children lolling dutifully over their school books.

Johnny sits gently stroking my hand.

'Are you all right?'

'Just glad it's over. It was a bit like someone playing Chopsticks on my ovaries.'

'You did really well.' He smiles fondly at me.

'Not sure it was my finest hour.'

'Maybe it'll be twins . . .' He grimaces, pausing to stare into space, awestruck. '*Christ!* Can you imagine?'

'Or maybe it'll be nothing,' I say primly, deferring to the gods, to fate. Metaphorically I roll my belly upwards to the unknown forces, like a submissive dog to its master. Just to make it quite clear I'm not taking any good will for granted. Not the time to risk provoking a lesson in humility.

'Only two weeks to wait.' He pats my hand. 'Though God knows, patience has never exactly been your forte.'

I think about the embryos tumbling inside, and fiercely crush down the bright flare of hope. *As long as I live, this is all I shall ever ask of you*, I think quietly, stealthily, so Johnny doesn't suspect the little prayer I'm constructing. *We're in your hands now.*

7

As we mark the days through that first week of waiting, Johnny remains unassailable in his optimism. Once or twice he saves a new IVF success story from the paper, and reads it to me over one of the meals he has once again resumed cooking. Then one night he returns looking troubled to say he has been asked to go to Paris for work. It's just for a few days, he explains anxiously, as we sit over supper that night. He will be back by the middle of the following week, in plenty of time to share the pregnancy test on Friday. He watches me hesitantly, waiting to see how I receive this news. But I reassure him I have plenty to keep me busy. Only that morning, I had accepted a commission that went some way to ameliorating the Dalai Lama debacle. A newspaper piece on Care in the Community I suspected must have come via Tamsin. As long as he's back for Friday morning, I say, it's probably far better that both of us should be kept fruitfully occupied.

For the first time the charity requests that tumble daily through my door demand attention. I find myself overwhelmed by the fragile nature of our lives. Blindness. Homelessness. Cruelty to children. Into all outstretched hands, I place little offerings of placation. One day on my way to work, I stop to help an elderly lady standing confused and frightened on the high street. She had been going to have her hair done, she tells me, when she had become disorientated, unable to locate any of the familiar landmarks. I drive her up and down the street urging her to call out when she sees the salon, but though she keeps up a series of cheerful anecdotes on growing up in the area, nothing we pass appears to prompt her fitful memory. I should be at a meeting, but over and over again we rejoin the one-way system, and I am just beginning to despair, when she finally recognises a friend at the bus stop who laughs merrily at our plight, and offers to take her there herself.

If I'm considerate to my fellow man, it can only help the balance book to tip, however fractionally, in my favour. Though the lifelong non-believer in me scoffs at the absurdity, at the craven expediency of such a notion, I frequently catch myself constructing furtive petitions to the heavenly adjudicator that presided over this balance book. Sometimes I employ base humility in my lobbying, at other times sly blackmail, and on bad days unabashed beseechment. Quite who it was who sat intently stooping over this book I wasn't entirely clear. As a student I had been greatly taken by Freud's suggestion that God was made in man's image rather than man in God's. And in reality I had never much shifted from this view. But now a curious knowing and not knowing became a habit of mind, a tricky doublethink of believing despite not believing.

And though I don't confess this to any one, even Johnny, my body is a temple now. No coffee, alcohol, raw meat or unpasteurised cheese. All food that passes my lips is chosen for its health-giving properties. Fruit whose fibre will weave tendrils around the foetus, vegetables whose folic acid will charge a tremulous heart into a beating drum of certainty.

That weekend we drive down to Sussex to stay with Tamsin and Pete, and after lunch we take a stroll with them through the woods that grow densely all about their house. Bluebells cluster between the trees, glowing improbably ultra violet. Pete carries the new baby strapped across his chest, while William, their eldest child, runs just ahead, whooping at the top of his voice, delighting in the echo and the occasional plump wood pigeon that startles up from the trees. The festive intensity of green, the sheer vigour of new growth weighting each branch, and the unaccustomed sweetness of the air all evoking an irresistible lightness of heart.

'How's your father taking it?' Johnny and Tamsin had fallen a little way behind. It was the first time I'd ever heard her broach the subject with him.

'My father?' Johnny sounded instantly guarded.

'Have you said anything to him?' she persists. It's the very question I haven't dared ask. After a reluctant pause, he shakes his head.

'No. No. Not yet.'

'What are you waiting for?' she asks gently.

'Good news, I guess,' he says, taking aim at the

bracken with a stick, and beginning to whistle through his teeth with a studied nonchalance.

Now the second and final week lies before us and Johnny must leave for Paris. At last I can count the days on one hand. He calls often, filled with solicitous concern. But the shoot is not going well. A series of logistical crises plague them and each day he sounds more miserable than the last. It looks as if he will have to delay his return, he finally confesses. He is sorry but he can find no way round it. He didn't need to elaborate. He knew as well as I that shame effectively held him hostage. His resolute refusal to explain why he was needed at home. But he promised solemnly he would make it back for Friday, the morning of the pregnancy test.

'Believe me, Rosie,' he says forlornly. 'It may seem small consolation, but you are in my thoughts night and day.'

So I promise to wait, urging him not to worry.

And maybe the truth is that I quite relish the prospect of being left to my own devices, to immerse myself without interruption in quiet anticipation. Sometimes I think of the slow dreaminess of pregnant women with a charge, a thrill that is almost erotic. That unconscious idle caress across the belly. The enigmatic inward smile.

Once, passing the closed door of the spare bedroom, I find myself retracing my footsteps, and pause to rest a tentative hand on the door knob. Since Johnny had finished decorating it, by mutual consent we had ceremoniously closed the door and never ventured there again. After a moment, my heart beating with a shallow flutter, I turn the handle, and step through the small rush of exhaled air. Johnny has sanded and painted the room into a heartbreakingly perfect shell and the smell of new paint has completely gone now. I stand looking about, surprised at the agitated rush of blood through me. It is the depth of *quietness*, the degree of *emptiness*, that is disturbing; the sensation they together produce of hopeful expectancy. Alarmed, I step out again, closing the door quickly, fearful of not keeping the sensation trapped inside.

I know I must strive now for equilibrium. Can see perfectly well how potentially damaging either too much optimism, or pessimism, could be at this delicate stage. But two such entirely different and irreconcilable futures stretch beyond the imminent positive or negative result that my imagination flicks restlessly between them, unable to settle on a resting place.

A positive result meant – what? Johnny and I with a small child at our side, the circle at last closing and fusing. While a negative result would surely leave us like an amputee, with an aching phantom limb.

Like a paranoid lover, my head scrutinises my body for telltale signs. But it's giving nothing away. Tender breasts signified – a flutter of forbidden hope bursts its way irrepressibly upward like a songbird – pregnancy! But hard on the heels of hope comes despair. Tender breasts mean, no . . . My mind blanching away, hope instantly souring. Tender breasts meant a period on its way. There are times, fleeting moments, when I quite genuinely fear for my sanity, unable to trust what is real and what is imagined.

As we inch our way into Wednesday, a terrible craving for alcohol seizes me. A longing for a soothing sedative to ease the ache of anxiety coursing through my veins. Because now I worry about worrying. All this adrenalin in danger of expelling the fragile seeds just as surely as if I downed a bottle of neat vodka. Tamsin calls with new attentiveness, the question 'Any news?' hanging unvoiced between us.

At lunchtime, on a sudden impulse, I stop at a travel agent's to enquire about long-haul flights. For a brief moment, the world and its possibilities unfold again before me, and feeling suddenly reckless, I reserve flights to Namibia. I think of an African village at dawn; the chatter of waking children and the call of a cockerel. I'm attempting to revive the old adventurous spirit. To have something before us that can leaven the disappointment if the pregnancy test proves negative. A compensation surprise for Johnny.

But in truth my heart's not in it. For I'm already rehearsing the phone call to the travel agent that explains regretfully I'm unable to go. 'I've just found out I'm pregnant,' I'll say casually. The joyful everydayness of those words. 'Oh yeh, by the way, Tamsin,' as if on an afterthought, when she calls, 'I almost forgot. The test was positive.' But with Johnny – with Johnny, I'll dance a savage celebration. And all will be right in our world again. A perpetual sunshine.

Please.

I stop and clasp my hands together, clenching my eyes tight shut.

Please.

Inwardly I prostrate myself, and for a moment think I may have glimpsed a transcendent eye opening attentively.

Please, please, please, I whisper.

But when I look again there is nothing. Only the non-believer with folded arms and sardonic smile.

Still hedging your bets? Who is it today then – our Heavenly Father or Lord Krishna?

I know, I counter quickly, seeking to placate by instant capitulation. *Tragic, isn't it?*

A quick ingratiating smile of self-mockery to dispatch her. Then slyly, just in case the prayer has been undone, one last urgent and heartfelt, 'Pleee-ease . . .'

I pause for a moment, urging the thought heaven-wards, sending it safely on its way.

'Hello there!'

I open my eyes to find the travel agent standing before me, with the booking forms in one hand. A complexion flecked by acne, and a suit so baggy it can only be borrowed, he stands tentatively poised between concern and amusement.

'Had me going there, you did! I was thinking – blimey, oh bloody riley, she's only gone and passed out on me!'

I gaze compassionately upon his blameless, unlined

face. *How little you know of life*, I think with infinite pity. *How much lies still before you.*

Harold is waiting on his doorstep for me, shifting uneasily from foot to foot. His round, haunted eyes and wild, white hair give the impression of a perpetual astonishment at all he surveys. He is dressed in stained trousers hoisted clown-like across the dome of stomach by threadbare braces.

'Hello there. Come in, come in.' A nervous chuckle at the back of his throat rumbling all the while. 'Come in, come in . . .'

As we pass through the hall, the door to the bedroom stands ajar. A stained bare mattress fills the tiny room, and a filthy blanket lies discarded on the floor. I follow him into a cramped sitting room, clustered with years of memorabilia. Old bottles of prescription drugs, seaside mementoes and black-and-white photos curling at the edges. He lights a cigarette and gestures me to a battered chair. I climb over the debris and sit tentatively, scanning quickly for a good setting for his portrait. Something that might suggest Harold's years in the community had not been so much about liberating him from institution-alised care, as abandoning him.

'I hope I'm not disrupting your day too much?'

He shrugs. 'Well, I usually just potter, you know. Maybe go down the community centre. Or just listen to me music.' A television sits unplugged amidst the clutter at my feet. He follows my gaze. 'Neighbour gave me that last year, they did. Lovely it was. Nice black-and-white picture when I got the aerial in the right place. My first telly. But I couldn't afford the licence this year. Had to unplug the bloomin' thing. 'Cause all me money goes on the fags, you see. Up in smoke like.' He laughs a great wheezing laugh that crackles and breaks in his chest. 'Yeh, all up in smoke.'

He spoke wistfully of his time in the mental hospital, though he couldn't recall exactly how long he'd been there. Fifteen years, he said uncertainly. Maybe more. He missed it though. It had been his home.

'So you've lived here since the hospital closed down then?'

'That's right. A good few years now. Yeh, a good few years . . .'

'Nice neighbours?'

'Oh yes. Very nice family upstairs. Very nice indeed. Very polite children they are. Very polite.' The ash from his cigarette tumbles unnoticed into his lap and speckles the cushions. 'I let the kids use the garden. Yeh . . . They like the garden, they do,' the nervous chuckle grumbling at the back of his throat. His childlike manner is curiously endearing I think, warming to him, glad he at least had the company of children to cheer his days.

'Would you like to see the garden? Never been much of a gardener, but I do me best. Yeh . . . Do me best I do . . .'

He hefts his weight from the chair, and rattles the

locks at the French windows, muttering and clucking as he struggles.

'How come your Christmas decorations are still up?' I ask curiously, looking at the faded tinsel draped across the picture frames, and the trailing fairy lights.

'Christmas decorations?' he says absently. At last the door swings open, admitting a gust of fresh air. 'Oh, the Christmas decorations! Well, saves all that fiddle taking them down and putting them up every year, don't it?'

And we step out into the radiant morning. Nasturtiums have seeded themselves everywhere and, though the garden is a mass of fleshy weeds, the orange flowers blaze on every side. I see immediately another potential picture. A powerful image in which Harold stands in the midst of all this vibrant colour, a dislocated figure, nonetheless shyly proud of his wild garden. An image entirely the converse in fact of what I first had in mind. What was it to be? A man liberated? Or a man abandoned?

'Don't know what they are. But they grow like billy-o.' He regards the nasturtiums fondly and leans huffing and puffing to pick up a pink plastic watering-can, discarded by the children in the long grass. 'Grow like billy-o they do.'

I set up the tripod amongst the straggling grass while Harold lights another cigarette, and stands impassively watching my preparation.

'Will me picture be in the paper then?'

'That's right.'

'What d'you reckon people round here'll think? When they read I was in a mental home and that?'

'Well . . .' I'm distracted, trying to get the legs level. 'Your neighbours know about your time in hospital, don't they?'

'Never had no reason to tell 'em,' he says frowning, a troubled look settling on his childish features, and releases the watering-can. I lean forward and give it back to him, its cheerful naivety the touching detail that makes the picture.

'Don't worry, Harold,' I say breezily, as I put my eye to the camera, impatient to get started. 'I'll make sure you look your best.' Though through the frame of my lens, he cuts a disconcertingly vulnerable figure amongst the festive flowers.

As I leave, the children from upstairs are playing on the doorstep, the eldest girl swinging to and fro on the garden gate.

'Is Mr Milligan famous then?' she asks coyly, eyeing the camera equipment.

'Famous?'

'Isn't that why you've come to take his picture?'

'Oh I see . . . Well, no. He's just — ' I'm thrown. The pictures weren't even developed and already the questions had begun. 'He's just seen a bit of life, that's all.'

The girl continues to swing to and fro, looking crestfallen. For a brief moment the day had taken on shinier possibilities. 'But will his picture be in the paper?' she persists.

'You'll have to ask him,' I hedge uneasily.

I set off up the hill as the alarm song of a blackbird swooping low across the gardens clatters on the balmy evening air. There was no doubt there remained all kinds of prejudices about mental illness. How *would* Harold's neighbours feel if they saw the article and his picture. What if they no longer trusted him with their children?

I turn quickly into the shabby post office. This was an assignment I highly valued. The first I could say that of for a very long while. I'd be crazy to jeopardise it. These pictures were going to be good. Very good indeed.

'Black-and-white licence is it?' the Asian lady behind the counter says in surprise, smiling pleasantly. 'Don't sell many of those these days.' I take the paperwork she hands me. On the other hand, there was no denying that to be found wanting the day before the pregnancy test would not be wise.

'Hello, photographer lady,' the little girl sings, still dreamily swinging on the gate. I knock at Harold's door, and after a moment he opens it and stands blinking in puzzlement at my unexpected return. I hand the television licence to him, then set off back up the hill. As gestures went, it was pretty unconvincing. Who exactly was I trying to fool? I pass a bin, DO NOT DROP LITTER, then further on another, missing half its sign, DO NOT. And without pausing to consider the matter further, or slacken my stride, I take the rolls of film and toss them into its yawning mouth. I'd just have to tell the picture editor that there had been a cock-up and the labs had lost them.

You wake early, knowing instantly it's the ordained day. You note with satisfaction that no period has arrived, and set off with determination to buy the test you've been too superstitious to allow yourself until today. Then you head for home again, the newly purchased pregnancy test now ticking like an unexploded bomb in your bag. And despite yourself, a larkish bounce now buoys your step. You know you promised to wait for Johnny, but it seems suddenly impossible you can wait that long. So you stop at the new organic café, thinking you'll just discreetly visit the ladies'. Gaily coloured banners flutter and twist across its cheerful facade. *Gala opening! Find it fresher elsewhere, we guarantee it must still be growing!* Shop assistants dressed as cheerfully coloured fruit and vegetables are milling to and fro, offering free fruit drinks, a slightly crazed atmosphere of revelry like a helium charge on the air. Already a crowd of passing shoppers are greedily snatching up the tiny cups.

The toilets are tranquil after the jubilant festivities outside. A quick inadvertent glimpse of your reflection in the mirror. Caught unawares, the face rears away with an expression that is furtively feral.

Trying to crush down the bright hope, you rip open the

plastic covering of the tester. Then willing your hand steady, you pee carefully on the stick. Almost instantly the test window shows a blue line. You wait for the second window. *Fifty-one, fifty-two, fifty-three,* the drumbeat of passing seconds rattling the vinyl walls. *Fifty-eight, fifty-nine, SIXTY.* The window is a blank. You bring it close to your eyes. You hold it far away. Maybe a trick of the light. Still time for a late chemical reaction. But the square remains empty. No line, no line. It has all been for nothing.

I push my way through the perambulating fruit and vegetables, blindly declining the flyers they proffer, calling up Johnny's number as I hurry. The carnival atmosphere a garish cacophony breaking about me. A giant chicken blocks my way but I grasp hold of its fluttering tail feathers, and yank it aside. Now a fluorescent banana takes its place, pogoing towards me, flapping its arms inanely. 'You don't have to be mad to work here, but it helps,' it gurgles in a kooky voice, then falls like a ninepin at my touch.

A negative result is at once no more than I had expected and yet directly counter to a quiet unacknowledged optimism that has nestled secretly in my heart of hearts all this while. All that science, all that money, all those doctors watching over us should surely have triumphed. I keep calling Johnny's number waiting for him to answer. And when he does, I find myself unable to speak. In the background, an airport tannoy clatters into life. But my silence tells him all he needs to know. He sighs deeply while I cry.

'Wait for me,' he says. 'I'm coming as quickly as I can.'

In a daze I kneel on the balcony, pulling up the weeds that thrust exuberantly amongst the flowers, the life force bursting irrepressibly forth from the gritty ground. Under each pot, framed by an earthy halo, teeming insects scrabble and writhe. In the old water-filled ceramic sink, the wriggling tadpoles are well on their way to becoming tiny frogs now. Why was it, when renewal was all about us, that we alone remained immobilised in this way?

I glance down at the street, hoping to see Johnny's cab turn the corner. A hollow-eyed girl is pushing a toddler in a pram, another baby on her hip. Behind her trails an older child, mouth agape, wailing at full volume, snail trails of dribble falling in ribbons from his chin. The girl turns her weary head towards him. 'Get your arse over here NOW!' Sick at heart, I reel away, clattering the French windows together in my haste to muffle their racket.

Johnny comes at last, dragging his overnight bag behind him. He looks gaunt and ill, as if he has aged twenty years. When he thinks I'm not looking he hastily pulls out a bottle of champagne he must have picked up before my call, shoving it unceremoniously to the very back of the larder. And we drive to the park, where we walk without exchanging a single word.

'How do you feel?' I ask after we have walked for some

time, sometimes sighing in unison. He reaches out helplessly, as if trying to pluck words from the air. He begins to speak, then falters. Begins and fails again.

'Empty,' he finally manages. 'Hollow to the core.'

Then he closes up like a clam shell, and the rest of the day passes in a daze. 'At least we have each other,' he says hoarsely before we go to sleep that night.

In the morning when I wake, it's as if I slip drearily up from cold water into cold air. *If I lie quietly*, I think, *I might feel no pain.* But even as I process the thought, a sorrowing is ebbing through me, a heavy torpor and dread at the coming day. I reach for the monumental effort of will it is going to take to lift my head from the pillow.

Johnny appears, hovering shiftily at the door. Dressed in work clothes, his eyes are shuttered, his farewell expressionless. On an afterthought he comes forward to offer a dutiful embrace, but it's like being taken into the arms of an undertaker. As he reaches the door again, I jump from the bed and run after him, sobbing, throwing my arms about him like a child, and he pats my back absently once or twice, as if in a reverie, before gently detaching himself and departing.

My face in the mirror is haggard. Shadows under my eyes, deep rifts between mouth and nose. The glittering eye seems to be closed today. I can't be sure. Willing it open. *If you grant me only one thing, one thing, let it be this. I shall never, never, ask for anything again – but don't, please don't, deny me the gift of life . . .*

But there is definitely no eye today. And straining to see in the shadows, I find only the non-believer again, watching quietly. I raise my hand to screen her.

Not now.

She smiles mockingly.

You're just whistling in the dark. You do know that, don't you?

No footholds to break my descent. The quicksands of thwarted longing sucking greedily at ankles, now knees, then torso, bearing me down to this nether land. The condolences of friends and family come from far away. I can't countenance Namibia, couldn't contemplate anything more than just getting through the day. We forfeit our deposit without a second thought.

While Johnny immerses himself in the distractions of the working world, I cancel all commitments and remain at home, scanning the clinic's literature, carefully rereading the charts that record their yearly success and failure rates. I feel insight into our predicament must lie hidden in their statistics, like some fiendish numerology puzzle. But though the factual basis of the figures should offer concrete insight, somehow they twist and turn like fiction. There are days when I cast amongst the numbers and find just cause to hope that if we tried again, we too must surely be admitted into the promised land which contained so many. Only to cast again and find instead a gloomy certainty that some mysterious curse meant we must remain forever excluded. On these days the feeling of being an outsider is like ashes in my mouth. On these days the papers and television appear filled with the smiling faces of women who clasp their offspring like competition trophies. The ease of their good fortune, the shininess of their lives, a lancing reproach.

The envelope is addressed in a neat hand. It is a while before I can bring myself to open it. *Yours in deepest sympathy, Anthony Ling.* I re-read it several times, exploring its concealed shades of reproach and disappointment, before finally setting it to one side. More than anything I had wanted to be a successful disciple. To prove capable of carrying the holy cargo to fruition. I take the portrait of his hands from my studio wall and put it away in a bottom drawer.

Whenever the opportunity presents itself, I take to covertly studying the children I encounter. It is their aliveness that transfixes me now. Hair renewing itself even as they go obliviously about their day, nails growing, small hearts invisibly pumping. And I see that this life force that sustains them is more mysterious and complex than I have ever comprehended before. All these years this daily miracle unfolding all about me and I too blind to see it.

I frequently brood now on my own family. How apparently effortlessly my mother had produced my three elder brothers and me. And they in turn their own five offspring. Each of us reassembled family traits anew; a certain vocal quality here, a distinctive shape of the eyes there, as if each of us was a freshly dealt hand from the same pack of cards. In particular, I often thought enviously of the brother closest to me in age who had

had a boy and a girl, one of whom closely resembled him, the other their mother, in a result so eerily neat it made me think of those dolls' house families you could buy in cellophane packets.

Sometimes we made my mother laugh recalling stories of our chaotic upbringing, and her struggle to maintain order amongst the shouting, unruly mob we formed. She had seemed overwhelmed by domesticity in those early years, her art school scholarship and early promise as a painter collapsing entirely under the onslaught of our demands. As I grew older I came to think of her as part of a cheated generation of women for whom education had opened avenues which the lack of career possibilities just as promptly closed again. Was that all that my own striving and ambition had been about then? Trying to make good her thwarted promise? How ironic for it now to seem that her achievements had, in fact, so far outstripped my own.

When my grandmother reached the age of eighty the family had held a party for her. Never much given to emotional declarations she had surveyed the three generations gathered before her with a flinty matriarchal eye before pronouncing her satisfaction at finding not a hare lip or a heroin addict amongst us. When she died, some years later, I had been greatly struck by the immortality this abundance of descendants so movingly embodied. The generations, as they streamed out of the crematorium, were a vibrant visible legacy. My father and aunt there to mark her passing, at their sides my three brothers, five nephews and nieces and two cousins.

Even in the midst of death, there was reassurance in the forward momentum of life.

But whilst this abundance had also almost certainly helped buffer my parents from our failure to conceive, Johnny's father had only him. When Johnny finally summoned the courage to confess our problems, his father would have no such comfort to draw upon. Nothing to soften the finality of staring down the barrel of his own mortality. It was no wonder Johnny kept delaying and delaying the moment when he must tell him.

In my face, I see age gathering like dust in the crevices. I am drying up. Tumbling headlong towards the gaping fissure of menopause. Might there really be no son or daughter beside me at the end? The long bracelet of generations broken. My passing no more than a step into quiet oblivion.

8

If work is a masquerade now, it's a useful one. Though I have to strive hard to maintain the impression of committed professional only so recently second nature to me, it's true that in the doing of a project, there are moments of forgetfulness, whole minutes at a time where I find I've been entirely distracted by the intricacies of the task in hand.

But today is a bad day. Some unexplained delay means I have nothing to do but sit idly waiting in the hotel lobby, and in the lull the sorrowing is ebbing through me again. I'm waiting to shoot someone called Bo Fisher. 'She's a famous television star,' Johnny had said when I told him I was about to turn the job down. 'It may not be as highbrow as you'd like, but it'll take your mind off things. Do you good.'

The lobby is one of those generic wood panelled ones, with an open fire, intended to indicate discreet English good taste. There was a period where I spent much of my time in hotels like this, waiting to photograph the latest celebrity, on the latest promotional round. I'd fancied my career might be going somewhere then. But I'd soon lost inspiration in the anodyne nowhere-land of the hotel bedroom. Quickly wearied of the stars with their blank eyes glazed by boredom or jet lag, and the hovering publicist who snapped at your heels like a worrisome terrier.

'Sorry, sorry! Running late!' today's publicist trills, appearing abruptly at my side. 'Bo's a little under the weather today. Been up all night with a teething baby. You know how it is.' She rolls her eyes in a humorously despairing gesture. 'So I've promised her, absolutely promised her, that you'll be in and out in half an hour . . .'

She feels familiar, though she appears not to recognise me. We exchange polite small talk on the way to the suite, and I wrack my brains, trying to place her. She is taking a call while I begin setting up, when suddenly it comes to me. Al Pacino. She had been his publicist some years ago, and overseen a shoot I had done with him. Here in this same hotel.

He had, I recall now, the day flooding back from some dark recess of memory, been unaccountably congenial, watching me work with interest. More accustomed to invisibility, to being just another faceless factotum in the marketing and publicity machine, I'd been unsettled by his scrutiny. But it had also emboldened me. And after a while, despairing of the pastel-coloured hotel suite, I'd suggested that we adjourn to the roof of the hotel to get some skyline shots. And greatly to my surprise, Pacino had readily agreed, despite the fact it had meant braving the cold, and navigating a steep rusty ladder.

This same publicist, now so immersed in her phone call, had been visibly put out at the departure from protocol. But she'd teetered up the ladder behind us on dainty kitten heels, close behind her the stylist, with clips in her mouth and a selection of outfits dangling from hangers, and behind them, Pacino's personal assistant, with a mobile phone in one hand and a laptop which struck the rungs as she climbed.

An icy wind was blowing, and the massed pigeons hunched in the eaves had filled the air with a velvet vibration, while the three of them stood watching us work, like resentful courtiers, stamping their feet and doubtless thinking of the warm suite left abandoned below. But all the while Pacino had remained astonishingly amenable, and I kept snapping away, knowing that as long as I retained the king's largess, I remained untouchable.

'We need birds in that sky,' I had said, half in jest.

'Who d'you think you are? Friggin' Annie Leibovitz or something? Jesus Christ!'

I hadn't been able to tell whether his deadpan tone was intended to indicate humorous approval or sharp rebuttal. But then he called casually over one shoulder.

'See up there, by the water tower?'

The publicist had stepped forward, nodding diligently, though her teeth chattered and her lips were tinged with blue.

'Climb up there, would you? And when I raise my arm, holler and shout, loud as you can . . .'

Pinch-mouthed, she had nodded stoically again and turned away. As the low winter sun set the city skyline alight, I had loaded a black-and-white roll for myself.

The magazine would never want this image. But I had known its worth, and in the privacy of the dark room intended to make it mine.

When the time came to bid him farewell, he'd clapped a bear-like hand upon my shoulder.

'Remember one thing,' he had said in his measured Bronx accent. 'Yesterday is *history*, tomorrow is a *mystery*. Today . . .' he had wagged an auspicious finger in my face, leaning close, 'today's a *gift*.' Then he had gathered himself, nodding sagely. 'Okay?'

Again I was unsure how humorous his intention was. But his heavy-lidded eyes appeared to express such intense sincerity, that I had nodded in a manner I hoped was appropriately touched and appreciative. Then he'd raised his hand in a theatrical salute, as if the credits were now rolling, and a film score swelling in conclusion as the door swung to. I had walked away down the long corridor, a little dazed by the dreamlike quality of the whole encounter.

And though the pictures the magazine had run of Pacino had been pretty standard fare, the black-and-white photographs shot only for myself had given me immense satisfaction. Emerging through the swirl of developer fluid, their strength had been instantly apparent. The one that pleased me most showed Pacino at the centre, his two assistants standing to attention, while above him the teetering silhouette of the publicist clapped her hands at the birds. The palms of his hand were raised like an imperious ring-master, head crooked to one side, a humour in the dry smile that made the gesture seem an ironic acknowledgement of the trappings of stardom that surrounded him. It must have been early January, the pigeons wheeling in the air behind him, and the evening sun just piercing the low-slung clouds along the horizon. For a while I had toyed with the notion of using it as a leaping point to gather a collection of photographs that explored the facade of celebrity, 'Celebrities Uncovered'. I'd even sent a copy to Pacino via the publicist, requesting permission to use it. But no response ever came, and the project, like so many others, had somehow languished.

But that had been in the time Before. Things were different now. Just keep it simple, I think, attempting to rouse myself from my torpor. The publicist's assistant puts his head round the door. 'She's on her way,' he mouths urgently, and the publicist brings her phone conversation to a crisp conclusion, just as Bo Fisher steps lightly through the door, close behind her her hairdresser and make-up artist.

'So when you said it was nothing to worry about,' Bo says, kissing the publicist on either cheek, and launching unceremoniously into the middle of what I presume must be an ongoing conversation. 'I was like, okay, cool. Nothing to worry about. But then I pick up a copy in the lobby. And I'm like, Oh-my-God!' She waves a magazine beneath the publicist's nose, before tossing it disdainfully to one side, and throwing herself carelessly across the double bed. 'I mean, Maeve. That photo is a disaster!' Her clothes appear to have been spray-painted onto her long limbs, and the attentions of her make-up team have given her a flawless perfection that startles the eye.

'What is it with those creeps, hanging out in the bushes, catching you all unprepared like that? What kind of day job is *that. Jesus!* I'm telling you, I'd happily torch the lot of them.'

'I don't think it'll do you any harm,' the publicist speaks soothingly. 'Quite the reverse in fact. Several people have called me to say they thought it a rather touching family tableau.'

Bo lights a cigarette and puffs frantically on it for a moment, seeming to digest this thoughtfully, her expression softening.

'Hello,' she says, turning unexpectedly towards me with an intimate and girlish beam. 'Are you ready for me then?'

She takes her seat before the camera, and the make-up team dart at her with quick dabs and tweaks, erasing invisible imperfections, while she struggles to get the cigarette to her mouth through the flurry of flying combs and brushes. Once this might have struck me as an opportunity to resurrect the book. A quick change of lens to get a wider frame or two of the hair and make-up team lurking like professional forgers in the shadows. But today – today I just want to get the job done and go home.

Her restless poses as I bend to the eyepiece are a series of stock smiles and coy head angles, the shutter clunking again and again in dreary collusion. A line from a catalogue that would never now be written comes fleetingly to me: 'It is this ability to mischievously undercut the elaborately constructed facade of the contemporary celebrity that so signally distinguishes Nichols from her contemporaries, and represents her most significant legacy to this much-debased genre.'

Then the publicist returns, tapping her watch, announcing Bo's car had arrived, and the team gather about her, clucking and fussing, sweeping her up and towards the door again. She is already cramming chewing gum into her mouth with one hand, while simultaneously pressing buttons on her phone with the other. 'Check you later,' she calls merrily, swinging her lovely blonde hair, and disappears through the door, her entourage in perfect step just behind.

I take up the copy of the magazine she has left discarded by the bed, and on the train ride home, flick through the crackling inky pages, noting despondently how indistinguishable the spooky artifice of its celebrity portraits are from my afternoon's work. It's a moment or two before I find the picture Bo had been complaining of. It's a slightly fuzzy snap of her strolling beside a handsome man who is holding a small boy in his arms. Walking just behind, caught in mid laughter, I'm startled to see Tamsin and Pete. All of them seem entirely oblivious of the spying eye of the paparazzi lens. I glance curiously at the text for explanation, something hauntingly familiar about Bo's companion.

Bo Fisher with her beau Kelly. Bo Fisher, 32, may have had a stormy romantic life of late, but it seems everything's happily back on track with on/off boyfriend, actor Bill Kelly. The couple enjoyed a stroll in the early summer sunshine with their one-year-old son, Noah, and friends. She side-stepped questions on whether marriage might now be on the cards, saying only: 'Becoming a mother has made me grow up overnight. I was 32 going on 17, but the moment you hold your baby in your arms for the first time, its amazing how everything changes!'

Of course. Bill Kelly. The beautiful lothario. Now with Bo Fisher, and apparently a father. He is glancing down at his son, and the stoop of his body, the very set of his face, indicates a touching tenderness for the child. A tenderness that sparks an alarmingly savage stab of longing in me. And though the grain of the picture smudges the detail I am seeking, I peer closely at the pixilated dots that form the little boy's face, something heartbreaking about his diminutive size dwarfed by the tall muscular frame of his father. I look back at Bill's blurred face, remembering how Tamsin asked us to look out for him in Vietnam, and Pete's tales of his compulsive philandering.

That's all it would take, I think, the dazzling pop of inspiration momentarily blinding me, like a flashlight breaking through darkness. One brief liaison with Bill. One quick illicit encounter. And then walk away having stolen the fruit of his loins and no one any the wiser. I smile bitterly to myself. At the absurdity of the notion. And throw the magazine away. I was clearly losing it. Not only childless but now demented.

But something about the notion lingers. In quiet moments the picture comes unbidden to me. I find myself furtively buying another copy of the magazine a few days later, a jumpy shame snapping in my throat. Was I losing my grip? *Was madness stealing upon me?*

And though I know perfectly well common sense should prevail, somewhere secretly I store him – or someone like him – as a shameful yet talismanic possibility that might keep options open, the thought of him inextricably intertwined with the touching vulnerability of the child held so gently in his arms. I tear the picture out, and stash it secretly in the inner pocket of my wallet together with the tiny print of Anthony Ling's hands. My back-up plan, my second parachute, if all else failed.

The first time she took me by surprise, sidling up against my legs when I was queuing in a shop. I felt the weight of her fall lazily against the crook of my knee. When I turned to look down, she had yawned and slid a small hand into mine. That was all. But I had felt a hallelujah chorus burst in my heart. She couldn't have been more than six then. A lovely grave face, her hair surprisingly fair.

A few days later, I had to retrace my footsteps having mislaid my mobile phone. Finding it beneath one of the chairs in the coffee shop I'd just left, I had hastily retrieved it, my panic giving way to relief. And as I straightened she was standing by the door, smiling. Everyone else was going about their business, but her eyes were fixed on me. This time she looked older, more like ten or so, and her hair had darkened with age. She rolled her eyes reprovingly, and I saw instantly how my propensity to lose things had become a running joke we shared. But by the time I reached the door, she had vanished again. How could I ever convey the urgency of finding her to Johnny? His concept of time was so unimaginably leisurely.

'I'm not saying never, okay? Just not yet. That's all. It's all still . . . still too raw . . .'

Often we found ourselves going over and over this same old ground, sometimes late into the night.

'I don't want our lives to be held to ransom by this, Rose. Don't want us to get poorer, and unhappier, chasing something for ever out of reach . . .'

'But it was you who first wanted children.'

'I know . . . I know that. And if they'd come easily, I would have been the happiest man alive. But . . .' And here he would pause, exasperated to find himself saying the same thing yet again. Weighting his words with renewed care. As if this time he might find a way of phrasing it that would at last make an impact on me. 'The statistics are against us, Rose. We have to face that.'

I should love him in sickness and in health. I tried always to remember that. And I guessed the secrets of his heart. Only needed to place myself in his shoes for a moment to understand. The whole process must have made him feel less than a man. The clinic so briskly stepping in to fill his biological role, reducing him to a mere bystander. His only remaining role to masturbate to order on a designated day. The sense of personal failure, and the bitter burden of guilt. All this, though he never spoke of it himself, I understood entirely, the knowledge cutting me to the quick. And yet – and yet here I was, the unacknowledged casualty of the whole sorry saga. Wasn't I due some understanding too?

Blame. That mean-spirited, unpleasantly shrewish word. I had always detested the self-pity it implied – forbidding it even in private thought, knowing perfectly well that even the slightest hint that I considered the whole thing his fault would diminish him beyond recovery. Would almost certainly bring a hasty end to our toppling marriage. But as he prevaricated, the ticking at my ear never let me forget that our chances dwindled with each passing month. And try as I might, I grew undeniably bitter.

Then, quite unexpectedly, perhaps sensing the precipice we teetered on, he finally, grudgingly, agreed. And the following morning, before he'd even woken, I'd filled in an application to extend our bank loan, and rung the clinic to set the whole thing in motion again.

Within weeks, a second box is dispatched to us. On its arrival I place it carefully by my bed, astonished at how differently I perceive it this time round. The fine silver needles and miniature bottles of hormones have become my allies, my passport to hope. Sometimes I sniff the Buserelin openly, familiarity making me casual now. Once in the middle of a shoot, catching sight of the time, I stoop low towards my bag and put the bottle quickly to my nose. And no one says a thing. It seems a way of life now. A way of travelling purposefully.

Once or twice I go to watch Anthony Ling lecture at the same place I'd first encountered him. He has an ebullient style that makes him popular, and his talks are well attended. I jostle in amongst the baby-faced students, helping myself as I pass to a sour cup of coffee from the vending machine. Just for old times' sake. Of course I understand very little of the technicalities he sets forth in those lectures. But I draw immense comfort from the breadth of his knowledge, and the precision of his certainty. There is a peaceful companionship in the close attention of his students, and the scratch of their pens as they transcribe his thoughts. I feel buoyed by the comradeship of fellow disciples. Yet both times, as I try to force my way through the throng of students that packs the corridor afterwards, he's disappeared before I can reach his side.

And now we've made the difficult decision to resume treatment, Johnny and I never mention the issue again. There seems oddly little to say. And even if there were, he is seldom here now anyway. These days he comes home later and later, smelling of smoke and alcohol, claiming pressing work commitments. Often I hear him stumble in long after I have retired to bed. And even when he is here, he appears distracted, immersed in the television or lost in private thought. Once or twice I make the mistake of asking if he's all right, and he answers with such ill temper that I resolve to leave him to his own devices. Why is it that the harder we strive for biological union, the deeper this emotional divide appears to grow? As if in direct and inverse proportion. I can only guess what dark thoughts possess him, or whether it is genuinely work commitments that keep him so late. But the shameful truth is that I am grateful for his distraction. I have no strength for passengers.

'What shall we do then?' I ask him one weekend, when for once we find ourselves at home together, the morning and afternoon stretching languidly before us. Having woken early, I have already tidied the flat and been to the supermarket while Johnny slept late. On the way home I'd dropped the box of newspapers and bottles off at the recycling bins, and collected an armful of dry-cleaning.

It's a translucently beautiful morning, the first true day of summer, air quickening in the new warmth, people out strolling with open optimistic faces, and I have caught their mood of festivity. In my absence, Johnny has risen from his bed, only to resume a prone position on the floor in front of the television, where he now lies, immersed in football highlights.

'Johnny?'

Still he doesn't turn, the light slanting in across his outstretched legs.

'What?'

'Shall we go out somewhere?'

An anticipatory roar from the football crowd, their distant klaxons sounding like passing ships. Merry birdsong from the trees beyond the window. Finally.

'*If you want . . .*'

Despite my good intentions, a scratchy irritation flares.

Since when had football exercised such a hold on him?

'Well, what do *you* want, Johnny?'

I move to and fro, snatching up the scattered newspapers he has spread all about him, clattering the discarded breakfast things, kicking up a commotion designed to raise him from his torpor.

'Since when have you cared about that?' he says sullenly.

And now the more I bustle about him, the deeper he appears to sink into paralysis, his eyes fixed unwaveringly on the screen. And the stiller he lies, the more ostentatiously I find I am bustling. I am reaching out to retrieve his empty coffee cup, when his hand shoots forward to claim it, clutching it to his chest with an absurdly aggrieved air, as if I am intent on stripping him of everything.

'I'm sure you can cope without me.'

'Fine,' I say, straightening, keeping my voice light. 'We've hardly seen each other for the last month. But if that's how you want it, fine.' I stop to snatch up the keys, feeling the air silken against my bare legs. 'Good thinking, Johnny.'

Still his attention remains locked upon the ebb and flow of the match, belligerent hostility even in his very stillness. A peal of sudden laughter from the street chides me with the gaiety of the day outside.

'Fine . . .'

I wait for him to attempt the last word but he seems to know that his silence is more hostile than any words could be.

With a sinking heart, I find I'm at the front door and hesitate, jiggling the keys between my fingers like worry beads. Can't think how to call a halt to this Cold War gathering with a momentum all its own.

Please, I could say, *let's enjoy this day together*. I could lie down beside him, fit myself around him. *Let's be friends*.

Yet pride holds me closed. There seems no way back, the impasse like a physical barrier. We had become a source of mutual reproach to one another. There was no denying it. A sensation of something oddly akin to homesickness sweeping through me.

'You're sure?' I call.

Even from the hall I can hear his exasperated sigh. 'I'm sure.'

I step out of the door, slamming it vengefully, and walk into the emptiness beyond, the angry bang resounding all the way to the street below. Glancing up quickly, I think I catch a fleeting glimpse of him at the window, pale as a ghost.

The visits to the clinic are the only appointments I prioritise in my diary now. Though I still take jobs, I do so only if I can make them fit around the ultra-sounds and check-ups. And the truth is, I would rather go alone. Rather not have Johnny as an occasional truculent attendant. What was the point when his heart was so clearly not in it?

Life outside the carpeted embrace of the clinic seems no more than a suspension until my return. Once the street door has swung to behind me, snapping out the rumble of city, I surrender with instant relief into its quiet internal flow. Nodding familiarly at the bored doorman, there is the quick decision whether to walk the four flights of stairs and arrive slightly out of breath, or take the lift and risk close proximity with another dazed patient, caught and spun by the same tortuous wheel of fortune. Once on the fourth floor, the hum of the coffee machine in the reception area, and the glimpse of the clinic coordinator through her half-opened door are my homecoming. I've read all the magazines on the coffee table from cover to cover. Know the infertility information pamphlets by heart. The nurses feel almost like friends now; their children, partners and minor ailments all familiar topics of conversation. And yet the more at home I feel, the more curious it seems that the women and sometimes couples that wait here, never acknowledge one another. Despite the common hopes that bring us, and the shared vulnerability that might bind us, we sit with eyes averted, feigning blind introspection.

One day I sit next to a woman, accompanied by a small boy. The child is greeted warmly by the nurses, and one of the embryologists on her way to the coffee machine stops to ask after him. They smile fondly in unison as he runs up and down, a maternal softness in their mutual gaze. *So he was conceived here*, I think, scrutinising him more closely. Perhaps this embryologist last saw him when he was no more than a collection of cells dividing under a microscope. I find I am both heartened by this reminder of the potential for success, and simultaneously envious of the woman's good fortune.

'Is this your first attempt since your son was born?' I ask, emboldened by the unselfconscious shouts of the little boy that seem to break the taboo on conversation. She barely meets my eye.

'Third actually,' she mutters in a toneless voice, turning away, and we sit in silence again, saved only by the cries of the small boy.

Perhaps the savage longing to be amongst the minority who succeed makes rivals of us all. Or perhaps, I think, shifting uneasily, it's more that each of us holds up a mirror to the other; the barren ones, ostracised from the human life cycle. We see a fellow outcast and avert our eyes in self-disgust.

Occasionally I glimpse Anthony Ling whisking away down the corridor. And once, I see him emerging from his office with a woman whose eyes are swollen and bloodshot. He is patting her consolingly on the arm, and saying something softly I don't quite catch. Another time I come across him standing in the corridor admiring a baby on a woman's hip. The woman's eyes shine with pride, the infant dressed as if for a special occasion, with a bow tied at a coquettish angle about her bald head.

'See how quick and alert she is!' I hear him exclaim with delighted satisfaction, as I pass by unseen. My invisibility seems only appropriate. We will meet again at the appointed hour. This time I must try harder.

In the doctor's consulting room, photographs of smiling babies cover the walls, many of them twins. It is the obstetricians' trophy space. Sometimes scanning carefully, my eye startles upon a set of triplets. An extraordinary abundance of life tumbling so hard on the heels of no life. A multitude of races smiling out at me. Chastising me for my failure to be amongst them. Once I would have dismissed the images of smiling babies as sentimental. Now they strike me as recording something impossibly rarefied, a whiff of the unicorn about them. I try to imagine the eyes of our baby smiling back at me from the wall. Why would I point my camera at anything else ever again? I would be compelled to keep on snapping. Roll after roll in wonderment. Our child fixed in emulsion a million times over, smiling toothlessly. Our hard-won union and fusion.

At some stage in our trials and tribulations, I bought a book on IVF written by a well-known infertility expert. Beneath the books on pregnancy and child care, one day I came across a small section for those cast out from this Eden and found it there, waiting for me. After reading it I passed it on to Johnny, who accepted it politely, before setting it unopened to one side. Sometimes I examine the author's photograph on the flyleaf, his moral and medical authority clearly embodied in the resolute set of his jaw. I had seen him occasionally on television, and warmed to the composed timbre of his voice, his confident proclamations a welcome bulwark against the shifting sands of uncertainty.

More often than I would like, I find myself taking up

this book, scanning obsessively for some new insight. Some sections offer me hope, while others dash me on the rocks of despair. Over time certain passages have become so familiar they've acquired distinct flavours as I read. Recently I've tried to get a grip and forbid myself the scary sections. One of the forbidden chapters is on how many attempts to make. Today I cheat and look quickly at it, my heart already jittery at what I know awaits me there.

> Clearly, it is not sensible to continue to have IVF treatment against all odds. Many women feel that they wish to gamble in this way, but they may be betting with their health and with their feeling of well-being. Infertile people, if they are not careful, can allow their treatment to destroy their well-being and to destroy the things and relationships they most value. It is unwise to let this happen to you.

The taste in my mouth is metallic, suffused with an unpleasant tang of Brussel sprouts. So I turn quickly to the paragraph that most bolsters me in low moments. Like a sugar lump after the spoonful of castor oil. I read it even though I have come to know it by heart.

> It is clear that, in general, the results of the treatment of male infertility using ICSI outstrip the results from all other treatments by IVF. From being a condition with the worst prognosis, male sub-fertility has now become one of the most successful to treat.

The lift of morale is palpable. The taste in my mouth transformed to zesty citrus. I scan it one last time before turning the page. *'From being a condition with the worst prognosis, male sub-fertility has now become one of the most successful to treat.'*

It was like the caress of a priest's soothing words. As I close the book, I pause before the great professor's picture for a moment. I know perfectly well that to genuflect would be absurd, yet the quick humble dip of my head is entirely involuntary.

Tamsin greets me at the door with Lily on one hip, her lovely face wan in the morning light, and when I ask if she's okay, she shakes her head wearily. I follow her into the kitchen.

'Bad night. Terrible night. Think she must be teething or something.' She shoehorns the small child into a high chair and passes a hand across her brow, momentarily closing her eyes. 'Packed Will off to nursery this morning, just to get a bit of breathing space.'

I contemplate the garden, and the litter of plastic toys lying scattered there. 'You want to get yourself back to work, girl.'

She smiles wearily. Though she's often complained of exhaustion, I have never seen her quite so drawn and ill.

She makes coffee while we chat inconsequentially about the foibles and fortunes of various mutual friends.

I wonder whether to tell her about my row with Johnny. Whether I dare confess the deteriorating state of our relationship in general. But she steadfastly resists any attempts to move the conversation my way, and as time passes I'm beginning to suspect an underlying purpose in her careful circumspection.

'Actually, there's something I've been meaning to tell you,' she says at last, getting up from her chair, and abruptly breaking eye contact. She begins heating milk in a shiny new saucepan and instantly I see exactly where all of this has been heading. 'You're not going to believe this . . .'

Inwardly I'm blocking my ears, cringing in readiness, praying for an instant deafness that might yet plunge the room into a profound and total silence.

'. . . but I seem to be bloody well pregnant again.' She keeps stirring carefully, feigning absorption.

'*Christ*,' I mutter, feeling a rigor mortis in the muscles about my mouth. 'How pregnant?'

'Four months,' she says, and finally looks at me.

For four months she has kept this to herself.

'*Christ*,' I say again. 'Lily's only nine months . . .'

'I know.' Her voice wobbles fractionally. 'It's a total nightmare. Pete reckons it must be an immaculate conception since we never have sex these days.'

I can't decide whether to sit down or stand up.

'I think we're both in denial to be honest.'

I can see she's torn between distress and knowing I'm not the right person to comfort her now. Has put off telling me for as long as she can, dreading the moment when it could be left no longer. I know her so well. And I want to show her how robustly I can take it. How infertility has not really made me so fragile my friends must censor their news. I'm casting around for something humorous to say. Something warm and compassionate. She needs support. I can see she's on the edge. But a creature lies writhing between us, flailing its arms, drumming its heels. *It's not fair!* it screams with the ugly glottal wail of a tantruming infant. *I trail barren wastelands, while here is Tamsin, bright seedlings springing so casually in her wake. Too much life, thoughtless life, an over abundance. I'm tired of suffering, weary of this exile.* The muscles around my mouth are so rigid it is physically impossible to form words.

She sits down, observing me with anxious concern. 'I'm really sorry,' she says softly.

I cannot bear this. Now she is dispensing sympathy to me. Then Lily starts yammering, reaching out for a toy she has dropped, and Tamsin turns quickly, grateful for the distraction.

'What's up, what's up, silly billy?'

It's as if I've been winded. I'm entirely bereft of words. Even I am shocked at quite how badly I seem to be taking this. Tamsin turns back to me, her voice breaking.

'I'm going to be one of those haggard women you see with hordes of snotty kids in the supermarket. Screeching like a banshee.' She attempts a smile. And I would too, if only rigor mortis would loosen its grip.

We walked side by side for so long. How did our fortunes diverge in this way? The lingering smell of fishfingers, the crayoned pictures on the fridge, the scattering of toys underfoot. Since William's birth three and a half years ago, it was as if a fug of domesticity had enveloped her, bearing her away downstream, while I remained on the bank, staring forlornly after her.

'It'll be hard at first,' I finally manage. 'But at least you'll have got it all over and done with.'

She sighs and shrugs, looking relieved.

'Apparently,' she says, rallying. 'Children born so close together are called Irish twins.'

My mouth at last forms the approximation of an appropriately sympathetic smile. 'You'll be fine.'

'I hope so.' She sighs again, stroking Lily's hair. The child looks back at her, a mirror-image reflection, the same dark eyes, the same bee-stung lips. 'We're just going to have to get on with it, aren't we, Lily Bugs?' The doting expression she casts upon her daughter triggers the twisting sensation in my gut again.

'Got to go . . .' I say, getting up abruptly. 'Bloody meetings back-to-back all afternoon.'

There are rows of shrunken coats and boots hanging in the hall and two miniature bicycles blocking the way.

'Is everything okay?' she asks, pausing at the door. 'Is it going all right?' She is trying hard, I think, wanting to acknowledge my troubles, whilst skipping deftly over their unfortunate contrast with her own.

'Oh yes, fine,' I say breezily, as if I've barely remembered we're undergoing IVF again. 'Like you say, you've just got to get on with it . . .'

'And Johnny?' she says tentatively.

'Oh, you know, getting off scot-free. Like they do. Typical man.' My carefree laugh fools neither of us. 'Listen, we're fine. Honestly. Worry about you, don't worry about me.'

She gives me a quick embrace, her eyes gleaming with sorrow.

A while back, when my aversion for the whole business of childbirth was beginning to wane and this consuming longing to take its place, I had forced myself to ask her the question that had come increasingly to haunt me.

'Do they make sense of life?'

I'd waited nervously, realising I was afraid to hear her answer.

'What?' She had asked frowning in puzzlement, since the question came from nowhere.

'Children. Do they stop you wondering what it's all really about? Make you feel, you know . . . fulfilled?'

'Oh God, Rose,' she had blown her cheeks out. 'Fulfilled?' She had laughed ruefully. 'Tired perhaps. Exasperated for sure. It's not a good day to ask.'

I had watched her closely, scrutinising her for secrets, as if I were standing on tiptoe, trying to look over into her world.

'Maybe you worry less about the point of life, because you're so God damn exhausted, you just don't have the head space any more.' She laughs. 'Who was it – Martin Amis or someone – described a baby as 'heaven and hell in a nappy'. Which sums it up pretty well, I'd say.'

I knew she was only partially telling the truth, choosing not to concede the moments of fierce private pleasure her children could stir in her. I'd glimpsed it in her face and tone of voice often enough, even if she wouldn't confess it now. The fleetingly enraptured expression of an adoring handmaiden. She was trying to protect me, I could see that, feeling both patronised and grateful at the same time. It had been a foolish question. Some strange compulsion to pick at the sore.

As she opens the door for me, she remembers that she saw some of my photographs in a magazine at the weekend. She says she knew instantly, without needing to read the picture credit, that they must be mine.

'I couldn't help feeling a pang . . . There you are, still out in the big wide world, you know . . . And here I am . . .' She gestures towards her thickening waist, and the snarl of bicycles and double pushchair that block the hallway. We stand surveying one another with a covert unease I realise has existed unacknowledged for some time now. Behind her in the kitchen, Lily starts up her yammering again. 'Good luck, Rose. Keep me posted, won't you.'

She smiles hastily, and the door closes smartly. I think of her turning inwards, new life quickening in her belly. Impossible to ignore the sound of churning waters. The stream separating us has become a river. I wouldn't call her again. Not for a long while anyway. There was no point. Sometimes life was about cutting your losses. Knowing when to move on.

9

The nurses keep a wall chart tracking each patient's progress throughout their cycle of treatment and my name hovers ever closer to the end. It's a road map I could walk in my sleep now. Having navigated the Buserelin-four-times-a-day stretch, I'm now onto the nightly injections home run. As evening falls, I take out the kit to prepare the needle. I'm awash with hormones. Pumping the stuff through my veins, I think. But I feel fine. I really do feel remarkably fine. It was true I'd had a sharp exchange with the cab driver on the way home. Some offhand remark he made about yuppies had struck me as being slyly offensive. And earlier in the day, perhaps I might have been a little tart with Gabriel when he'd called me in a rather giddy state to announce he had – once again – finally met the man of his dreams. But on the whole it's surprising how incredibly normal you can feel on this stuff.

And I'm sitting on the bed, with the implements laid out before me, when I hear Johnny let himself in at the front door. He mutters some kind of muffled greeting, then goes on into the kitchen. Twice I call him, and twice no answer comes. I hear the sound of the fridge door as I attach the fine silver needle to the plunger. I hear the pop of a cork being pulled while I draw the liquid hormone up into the needle. Then the tinny merriment of audience laughter from the television as I drop the syringe into its casing, and the click of a wine glass being set down. How odd and lonely this little ritual feels tonight. I prime the syringe, and placing it against the bare skin of my thigh, press the button. It's the work of a moment. I call for Johnny again. Still no answer. And wipe away the pinprick of blood.

In the kitchen, I find him sitting hunched over his phone, a deep frown creasing his brow. '. . . that's all I ask. Take on board their feedback, for Christ's sake. We're all expending needless energy here . . .' A long pause while he listens intently. A scratchy irritation prickles up like heat rash as I keep him in my peripheral vision, moving around the kitchen, tidying away the day's debris, wiping the cloudy surfaces. Whatever this work crisis is, it's clearly his first priority.

At last the conversation ends and he pushes the phone away, his head falling into his hands, a weary exhalation whistling forth long and low. He's obviously under enormous pressure, I think. Best to say nothing. Now is not the time. Yet my mouth forms the words unbidden.

'Didn't fancy playing Florence Nightingale then?'

He appears not to hear.

'Johnny.'

'Hmmm?'

'You didn't come when I called. I was doing one of those injection things. You know, you have to stick a needle in your leg. According to the clinic some husbands insist on giving it themselves.' The sarcastic laugh rattles unpleasantly in my throat.

'Oh, really . . .' He glances quickly at me, taking me in for the first time, then reaches for his mobile again. 'Well, you know me. Always been a bit feeble when it comes to needles.'

I begin making coffee, trying hard to keep my voice light.

'Well, I'm not too fond of them myself.'

He begins tapping out a number, while I measure coffee in spoonfuls. *One. Two. Three.* Something sour and aggrieved quickening in me.

'I mean, far be it for me to upset your delicate sensibilities, but I wouldn't mind a bit of moral support now and then you know.'

He stops dialling and looks up again with a distracted expression.

'I'm not sure I understand the problem. I mean, I'm here, aren't I?'

I'm about to speak when I find instead that I have begun to cry. Bitter tears that spring as if from nowhere, apparently revealing a deeply felt but hitherto unacknowledged wellspring of resentment.

'Well, from where I stand it seems like this whole thing's down to *me*!' The *me* punctuated by a crash of spoons and cups, a clattering of kettle; a domestic timpani spangling beneath my fingertips. '*Me* whose got to stick all these needles in my leg. *Me* whose got to snort all those chemicals . . .'

I glimpse Johnny's goggling face watching in astonishment, and the goggling goads me beyond endurance.

'I mean, the least you could do. The fucking least you could do is hold my hand once in a while . . .'

Then my mouth sags at the corners like a Greek tragedy mask, a wetness of tears flooding my face, my nose running too now. I'm awash with self-pity. Johnny sets his phone down and comes towards me, his fists clenched in fury.

'Jesus Christ, Rose! This is what you wanted, isn't it? *Isn't it?* It's hardly as if I twisted your arm.'

I'm hyperventilating sobs, astonished myself at the sheer theatre of it all. 'Just get involved, will you? That's all I'm saying. *Get involved!*'

He stands regarding me with an expression of despair. 'Look at you. Look at the state of you, Rose. All those hormones have just tipped you over the edge . . .'

A sudden silence. The heart-stopping hush of the moment before a falling object strikes the floor. The undeniable truth of his diagnosis, together with the shirking of personal responsibility it seems to imply, slowly sinking in. Then a low rumble that rises in a whistling crescendo, pushing aside major organs as it plumes, my body no more than a conduit for this hormonal fire and brimstone.

'Jesus Christ! There you go again! Sounding like some fucking bystander. Do you think I want to be walking around like some . . . toxic health hazard? Do you think I enjoy being pumped full of this crap? I mean, doesn't it ever occur to you that none of this has anything to do

with me? That I'm not the one who's infertile, Johnny.
YOU ARE!'

The rage still firing through my limbs, rattling my
very bones now. I slam the coffee pot away, splashing
black gritty grounds across the wall, a savage flare of an
exhilarated and dizzying horror at the unleashed words.
Flying past him for the door, I catch a fleeting impression of his face, ashen and appalled.

He comes to bed much later. I hear him undress, feel the
dip of the mattress as he lies down. But I feign uncon-
sciousness, and after some time I hear from the rhythm
of his breathing that he has slipped quietly into sleep.
The next morning, when I wake, the bed beside me is
empty. The kitchen too. No sign that he has ever passed
this way in its spick and span orderliness.

I had finally said the unsayable. It had been unforgivable. Quite the most brutal thing I had ever said
to anyone. I stand at the door listening intently to the
silence.

At least there was no longer any pretence. I was on my
own now.

The midnight injection tonight. The last signing off
before the flurry of operations, then the tortuous
Long Wait all over again. When I broke the icy silence to
tell Johnny I would rather go alone, he had shrugged.

'Suit yourself.' And whistled tunelessly through his teeth, in the way he always did when he wanted to make a show of indifference. 'Whatever.'

I light candles, and line them along the mantelpiece. The air fills with the acrid smell of sulphur and a sudden longing to see Anthony Ling flares like hunger. But if I were to call him, what would I say? I take out the little photo of his hands from my wallet and prop it behind the dancing candles. I never did give a copy to him, I realise, looking intently upon it. But I could easily remedy that this evening. He lived so close to the hospital, it would be the work of a moment to push a copy through his letterbox as I passed by.

Hurrying across the dark high street, I step carefully over the outstretched hand of a young girl lying fast asleep in a shop doorway, and pause briefly to slide a ten-pound note beneath her makeshift pillow. The streets are already emptying, just the occasional person hurrying to their Friday night rendezvous. I pass a pub, the swell of laughter and music spilling out on to the quiet evening air. Then striking left, I turn off the brightly lit thorough-fare, plunging into the lovely rustling affluence of his leafy square.

One of his sons opens the door, dressed in crumpled pyjamas.

'Dad?' he says. 'No, he's not home yet. Maybe later.' He shrugs unhelpfully.

'Who is it?' That woman's voice again, calling.

'Nothing. Just a package.' The boy stretches out his

hand to take the envelope from me, but I keep a firm grip on it.

'I was hoping to give it to him in person, you see . . .'

He shrugs again, slouching in that exhausted way some teenagers have. He looks more like his mother than his father, I think resentfully. He watches me morosely, and shifts restlessly again. I step away, bidding him goodnight, the door slamming almost instantly in my face.

I should go straight to the hospital now. It was enough to have come this far. It would be odd to wait for him. I'd look a little furtive hovering here with my envelope. The neighbours might get uneasy. I stand by the garden wall, peering up at the dark windows of the house with a gnawing, thwarted sensation.

Then, without forethought of any kind, I launch myself at the wall, succeeding after a perilously uncertain moment in hefting my weight up and over, coming to rest with both legs neatly akimbo. Astonished laughter rises in me. Sometimes, *in extremis*, you could find yourself doing the oddest things. But as long as you knew that it was strange, as long as you meant no harm by it, it wasn't the worst thing in the world. Somewhere close by, coming fast down the high street, a police siren soars into the night, instantly extinguishing my amusement. I glance quickly towards the house again. Only reflections of the trees, and a series of refracted new moons in the top floor windows. Taking care not to crease the envelope, I ease myself down into the dark garden.

The sensation of trespass, of standing on soft earth I have no business to set foot on, sobers me still further.

As my eyes adjust I'm beginning to trace the shapes and outlines of the garden, and in the half-light I can just make out the glimmer of an ancient tree, heavy with flowers, at the end of the lawn. Crouched beneath it, the scent is overpowering, the sweetness of the flowers charged, even in my fearful state, with a delectable headiness.

At one of the windows there is a momentary flash of movement. A brief glimpse of Anthony's wife as she pulls a curtain to. Then a hush so deep you could fall forever through it. As I sink to the ground, the wind stirs the tree above my head, blossom showering me like confetti. Time passes. The sound of a cistern being flushed. Then lights go out. First one, then another. Quite soon after, a third. The family all apparently abed. Then once again, nothing. Time torturously slow now. Finally . . . finally a car drawing near. Stopping. The jingling of keys, and then the front door closing. I wait, ears on fire. Here he was then. *What now?*

After a moment, the sound of the back door being unlocked, an impatient rattling at the latch, some sixth sense apparently alerting him to my presence. The scent of flowers is the rank smell of fear now, my scalp tightening like shrinking cling film, hair roots on fire.

I step back into the darkest, coolest recesses of the tree, right back where the crook of the garden wall is clogged with damp leaves, and hunker into the ancient peaty stench. Then the garden door scrapes open and Anthony Ling appears, a struggling cat held fast under one arm. It bolts from his arms, and he disappears again, leaving the door ajar, before reappearing with a drink. He pulls up a garden chair and sinks wearily down. I catch the sharp clink of ice as he sips. Once or twice he sighs. My heart begins to slow again, and at length I realise we have lapsed into an oddly companionable silence.

Our situation is without doubt a bizarre one. With my heels sinking in leaf mould, and pins and needles dancing in my legs, I could hardly deny it. Yet where else should I be tonight? The pubs and restaurants I'd passed were filled with friends and lovers conversing and flirting. While here I sat with a man who, though I scarcely knew him, was the potential pollinator of our children, our only viable conduit to life. Momentarily the weight of eggs in my belly shifts and fades again. In just over thirty-six hours, everything would once again reside in his hands. We were so adrift from the natural order of things, I had no social code of practice to navigate by any longer. I could rise up and step forward, apologising profusely for my trespass, and hand over the picture, but I see now it was not words I have come for. Just to rest a while beside him. That was all I required. The swirl of evening air between us, the cat unexpectedly rearing through the gloom to roll and rub at my feet. All about us the roar and rustle of the city, and the sappy crackle of the garden as it grew.

At last he stands up, staggering slightly at the stiffness in his limbs, stretching and yawning, heading towards the house without a backward glance. In the half-light I glance at my watch. Nearly midnight. After a moment, I rise up too, staggering at my own bloodless legs and,

with a hammering heart, scale the wall and set off at a
half-run for the hospital.

This time, once the embryos have been placed
safely inside me again, I cancel all work commitments and take to my bed. Daren't risk anything that
might be grounds for later self-reproach. Last time I
hovered too hesitantly on the brink. I've gone over my
tactical errors many times. The body can tell when the
spirit is tentative. And having cut my ties from the world,
I embrace the two-week wait without compunction.
No other purpose now than this.

Our shopping is delivered, where it remains clustered
in the hall until Johnny returns in the evening to pack
it all away. And an agency cleaner comes twice to clean
and tidy the flat. To my relief, her English isn't good
enough to ask what ails me, though once or twice I
glimpse the glitter of her curious eyes through the crack
of the door as she passes to and fro.

Though last time there had been twelve eggs, this
time, standing in the shadows of the operating theatre,
Anthony Ling had called out a total of only eight. Like
water dwindling to a trickle, just as I'd always feared.
Before I'd gone to sleep that night, I'd placed his
photograph beneath my pillow. And like a sorcerer he
had set to work and conjured life again. The following
morning, five eggs had successfully fertilised, and they

had replaced two, and frozen the remaining three.

As the two weeks wears to its weary close, I bargain endlessly with myself as to when I can purchase the pregnancy test. I visualise buying it from the chemist, a furtive thrill at the prospect, a marker nearer.

When Johnny asks if he should keep the day of the pregnancy test clear, it strikes me that this is the first direct question he has put to me since the night of that terrible row. The ground between us is now so fragile that all conversation has been pared to a bare minimum of primly polite exchanges on mundane domestic matters. And even then we speak without making eye contact, our faces rigid masks of constraint. More than anything, it is the fastidiousness with which we adhere to this new formality that reveals how very deep our estrangement has become. I thank him politely for the offer, but say I don't really see much point. What will be, will be. Probably best just to treat it like any other day, I shrugged.

'Okey-dokey,' he nodded with what I took to be relief, and went away whistling through his teeth again.

The weight of emotional and financial investment that lay behind us propelled us irrevocably on towards this last attempt. Always this tormenting possibility of a happy conclusion like a phantom just beyond our fingertips. But if we failed this time, there would be no more chances. It would be the end of hope. I could no longer remember a time before this longing. How would we make sense of our lives?

*　　*　　*

And now at last, the penultimate day, though my body is giving nothing away, the old feeling of being merely a head atop an inscrutable torso returning. For the first time in two weeks, I venture from the flat and buy the pregnancy test in a joyfully mundane transaction, the package disconcertingly light, as if its slim cellophaned shape contained nothing more than hope. Tomorrow I could use it the moment I woke. I have no concept of what the day beyond might hold – sorrow and joy offering such entirely opposing scenarios, I can envisage neither.

But the next morning, coming instantly into consciousness, I know even before the room has come into focus that there will be no need to unwrap the little packet lying ready beside the bed. My period has come. The familiar low heaviness in my belly could have no other cause. The relentless cycle has continued unimpeded, briskly expelling the precious cargo.

Johnny is in the kitchen, gulping coffee down, looking out of the window with a pensive expression. I flick the rumble of radio off and he spins round to greet me, apprehension widening his eyes. I find I can't speak. Instead I stand motionless, watching the colour drain from his face.

'Bad news then?'

I nod and he takes me in his arms, and we stand for a long while, mutely swaying.

I lie alone with the windows shuttered. The passing cars sound oddly muffled. Often, away in the kitchen, the phone rings shrilly, and sometimes my mobile too from somewhere close at hand. Johnny had had to leave hastily for work, promising to be back as soon as he could. He'd probably alerted Tamsin. And she would probably have alerted my mother. And maybe Gabriel too. The ringing appears to come from another planet, I think indifferently. A maddening and irrelevant sound. There they were out in the faraway world of sunlight, like a noisy flock of alarmed starlings. The shadows across the room grow longer. Occasionally I move slightly to let the blood flow through when numbness in a limb becomes unbearable. My sighs are loud and disconcertingly close. Yet I have the hallucinatory sensation they come from someone else. I am only watching the shadows, the rest of the room and its contents veiled to me.

At length I hear the front door slam. After a moment the bed dips as Johnny sits down beside me, out of breath. Still I don't move, keeping my back to him. My foetal position is locked now, curved like an armour-plated armadillo. He strokes my back tentatively, and then my hair, before drawing me hesitantly to him. I will remain impervious, I think as I fall towards him: yet I'm startled by the sensation of homecoming as his arms close about me.

'Hey, hey, hey. Come on, Rose, don't. Don't beat yourself up like this,' he says softly, his voice so thickened by emotion it might be the voice of a stranger.

When I look into his face it is as if I am seeing him, really beholding him, for the first time in a very long while. A lock of hair falls across his forehead, grazing the sad downward sweep of his eyes. I see how lines have formed, and wonder at the vanishing years. Once his eyes were a fever-bright blue, now all the colour has leached away. He takes my face in his hands, his jaw tightly clenched.

'I'm so sorry,' he says fiercely, spilling sudden tears. 'I'm so sorry, Rose.'

I wipe the tears away, astonished.

'Don't say you're sorry. Please, don't say you're sorry.'

He continues to weep, noiselessly, pressing his face to my shoulder. I'd never known him cry before. All this time I have wondered how it was he felt so little. The blood-like warmth of tears is soaking through to wet my skin. After a while, he sits up and wipes his face angrily against his sleeve, struggling to compose himself.

'The stupid thing is, Rose . . . I always just took it for granted that we would have children. Just assumed that that would be the natural progression of our life together. We met. We got married. Then it all just . . . I never thought in a million years . . . I mean . . . What kind of man can't give his wife a child?' He attempts a laugh, but the exhalation of sound he makes is more an angry choking. I try to hush him, but mute for so long, he is unstoppable.

'I suppose I always wanted the relationship with a child that my father never had with me. I look at these hands . . .' He cups them in a gesture of supplication, '. . . and I think no one will ever have hands like these again. All that knowledge, all that wisdom I dreamed of one day passing on. There's nothing in front of me now. Just an emptiness . . .' The phone is ringing again now, insistently on and on, but he seems not to hear. 'I went through a phase of dreaming about dead babies . . . It's insane, I know. I would have this dead baby in a pram, and people were coming up to me, and I had to keep explaining it was dead over and over again.' How could he never have spoken of these things, I wonder anguished? 'Often, when I'm out walking. Just, you know . . . going about my day . . . it's like this phantom child is running ahead of me, just out of reach.' I nod in recognition, unable to speak, a terrible tightness compressing my heart. 'It's the saddest thing, Rose, to think that child will only ever exist in my head.' I nod again, finding I am crying as well now. He drops his head to his chest, too overcome to continue.

I entwine my arms around him, pulling him to me with my legs, impaling him with fierce kisses. Beloved Johnny. If I had harboured resentment towards him, it is wholly extinguished by this revelation of despair.

Our lovemaking is tender; his touch at once new, and yet deeply known. 'I've missed this . . .' he whispers, as we cling together. 'Missed you . . . So lucky to have you, Rosie . . .'

We lie like this for a long while, until I see that his eyes are lustrous in the half-light, weariness making them heavy. Then the sorrowing comes back, like a black ink flooding through me. And as he drifts into sleep, my head is clearing. Suspended in that deep freeze. Three clusters of existence.

I roll in closer to him. I have no choice. He's open to me now. Though even as I speak I know it's risky, the moment fragile.

'Johnny,' I say low in his ear, a lover's silky wheedle. 'Can I ask you something?'

His interrogative assent is unguarded, abandoned as he now is in this half-sleep.

'How would you . . . how would you feel about giving it one more go?'

'What? Give what one more go?' he asks drowsily.

'Those embryos . . . remember . . . the clinic froze three embryos for us.' I feel his body startle into instant wakefulness again.

'Jesus Christ, Rose, we've only just . . .' He pulls abruptly away, swinging upright. I wait, watching the stoop of his shoulders. If he refuses, it's all over.

'Please, Johnny . . . Please. We don't have to give up just yet.'

He sits for a long while, his hands covering his face, the ticking of the alarm clock the only sound in the room.

'The odds are against us, Rose. Why put ourselves up, only to be shot down in flames all over again?'

'Please . . .'

He remains quite motionless, his hands still clamping his face, before at last seeming to reach a decision and straighten again.

'Okay,' he turns to address me, his voice leaden. 'Okay. One last time . . .'

'I swear, I swear.'

'I mean it, Rose. One more, and *that's it*. And if it doesn't work, we walk away knowing we have given it our best shot. Otherwise this thing will simply destroy us . . .'

'Thank you,' I say, clasping him to me, relief and dread, sweetly bitter in my mouth. I nuzzle close, burying my head. 'Thank you, thank you, thank you.'

On my way to sign on with the clinic again, a blind woman led by her guide dog boards my underground train. With an almost audible exhalation of sympathy, the massed commuters shuffle aside, making generous space for her, and a businessman leaps eagerly to his feet to offer his seat. But the woman shakes her head, declining. A few stops on, she loses hold of her strap, and someone else stretches out to guide her hand back. 'Here you go!' Again she shakes her head, snatching away her hand, and turning her back to the carriage. At her feet her guide dog gazes unblinkingly as if into a mirror, at the massed commuters who gaze with cow-eyed sentiment upon him. As the woman prepares to get out at her stop, a ruddy-faced businessman calls out, 'Do watch your step there, won't you!' She springs nimbly onto the platform, before turning sharply to address us through the diminishing gap in the doors. 'Might I suggest you just concentrate on watching yours.' Then the doors hiss closed and the train picks up speed again. I catch a last whip pan glimpse of her with her head held high, striding regally up the platform as the dog loyally bears her forward.

And somehow the episode clarifies something. As she

disappears from view, I resolve that we will tell no one about this last and final attempt. As much as anything, I see I've come to dread the kindness of friends; their gentle compassion only underscoring our interminable exile from their easeful world.

M y IVF book is so alarming about the potential long-term health risks to babies conceived from embryos that have been frozen, that I at last set the slender volume to one side, and resolve never to open it again. Denial is my new ally. But at least there are no drugs this time. No operations to endure. Johnny has finally explained everything to his boss, and is always by my side now, the two of us waiting like old pros, keeping our distance from the nurses with their cheerful chatter, and our eyes carefully averted from the mask-like faces of the other patients. In the days that follow the transfer of the three embryos, we are solicitous and careful with one another. And I dare to hope that this new geniality is exactly the rich compost into which fragile seedlings will at last put down roots. After two weeks we take the pregnancy test, and wait again. Always waiting. And then . . . And then the test is negative, and on the instant I am tumbling headlong through the blank window of that tormenting tester stick, despair blotting out the world.

It is as if, with a chill wind at my throat, a great wasteland now opens up before me; an Arctic wilderness that is immense, daylight sliding away even as I gaze upon it, into the melancholy onset of a night without end.

What was the point of it all? The mocking question, undulating up from the depths to whisper ceaselessly in my ear now. And with a clarity that cuts like a knife, it comes to me that our failure to conceive might not be a case of random misfortune at all. That it was in all probability, more a failure to have *merited* it. And that if I hadn't merited it, it was because of my undoubted moral weaknesses, chief amongst them my failure, for all those years, to value the thing that really mattered. My sins crowd in upon me now. The gift of life. Unrecognised by me for all that time. And what was it that had blinded me for so long but self-absorption? And ambition? Investing in the wrong thing had consequences. Really it was perfectly obvious. Hard to believe I'd never seen it before. There I was paying the clinic to attend to the body, when all along it was the soul, *the soul* that was wanting. And now I see the error of my ways, I repent. On bended knee, with heart ablaze, I truly, truly repent.

Johnny received the news of this final failure like a man who has his last stay of execution snatched away. But I can see at once, it's no more than he expected. He holds me close, urging me to focus now on the things we have. To stop pining for those we don't. He has put together some crazy plan for us to sail around the world together, and thinks we should discuss it further when we've had a chance to digest our disappointment. 'I suppose I've been going through this incredibly painful and gradual dawning,' he says wretchedly, 'that this was just not meant to be. That you can only play with the cards you've been dealt in life.'

In vain I try to persuade him. In vain I lobby. One last final attempt. One last bid for salvation. A baby would give our lives purpose, I pleaded. A baby would bring a kind of immortality. The vigour of the limbs, the crooning song, all heralding a meaning to life in one dear form. Yet despite my tears and protestations, he remains adamant.

'What about your father?' I ask desperately, reaching for the only card I can think of left to play.

'I've spoken to him,' he says flatly. 'We had a long talk. He was gutted on our behalf. But he understands we must move on now.' There is such finality in his words, it is clear the subject is now closed for him. A piercing loneliness strikes me: I see that all this while I have clung to hope, he has been on an entirely different trajectory letting hope go. And that his resolution, now arrived at, cannot be reversed.

'Is it really so impossible for you to imagine a life that is just the two of us?' He rakes his fingers through his hair as if to wrench it from its roots. 'Jesus Christ . . . What's to become of us, Rose?'

On and on the arguments and bouts of pleading, until at last, exhausted, he slams his hands on the table.

'Okay. That's ENOUGH! *Enough* . . . I've ruined everything for you. Don't you think I can see that.' He stumbles to his feet, sending cutlery and glasses clattering. 'The truth is . . . The truth is you'd be far better off without me. You know it. I know it.' Our eyes are locked, a terrible trembling overtaking my limbs. 'Well, you have my blessing. Leave me. Go. Go and find a man who *can* give you what you want.'

On this note we retreat to different rooms and later separate sleeping arrangements. I lie awake late into the night, flayed by the savage yearning to resume the treatment. Then, at least, we had had hope. Then, at least, we had travelled side by side. Nostalgia dogs my waking hours and colours my night-time dreams. And now, instead of angry words, all communication of any kind simply ceases.

There seems no way back and no way forward. Should I stay, or should I go?

In the days that follow, I take to driving. Up and down, to and fro, a random criss-crossing of the city's highways and byways. There is something numbing in the apparent purposefulness of the car's motion. Even in my dazed and inert state, the almost imperceptible foot pressure can propel me through time. Minutes slip away, whole hours, while the radio chitter-chatters blandly on. Grey road signs, grey street lamps; a monochrome city. There had been nothing ennobling about our sufferings. No spiritual redemption. Wherever I look, I see litter flapping in the hollows and crevices, fly posters peeling from their hoardings, decay and neglect powdering the buildings to dust. There was no heavenly court after all. No sense, no meaning. Just brutally random events. I visualise wiry marsh grass poking its way up through the gutters, the swamp lands that once lay below bubbling up. I feel the tremble of the pavements as they teeter and fall inwards, the secret rivers underneath running grey like mercury, sweeping everything away.

Anthony Ling's name is in all the papers that morning. A white woman has given birth to black twins, and everywhere I look there are scare stories about mix-ups in the labs, in which he is widely quoted as an international authority on IVF issues. I had expected him to cancel our meeting, but here he sits, listening quietly, occasionally offering a fresh tissue when the last becomes too soaked in tears.

'For all my patients,' he says, when I have finally finished explaining our sorry tale, 'this is probably the toughest decision of all. Whether to walk away, or give it one last shot. Over the years, I have come to realise that in our quest to help couples conceive, we can all too easily forget the importance of helping them move on. And the apparent miracles that reproductive technology appears to promise can make this immensely hard. I understand that. It seems to offer the fulfilment of all our longing, if only we are willing to try hard enough.'

I nodded, dabbing my eyes. It was true. We had come seeking absolution. The money, the discomfort, all seemed part of the penance. We had observed the pre-scribed rituals to the letter, believing it could surely only

Rebecca Frayn

be a matter of time before our prayers were answered.

He spoke with the same calm fluency that had always exercised such a powerfully soothing effect on me, though this time I saw he was gently closing the door he had for so long held ajar. 'Accepting the condition of childlessness is undoubtedly a painful and difficult process. Yet for many patients, after a period of mourning, it is the start of resuming a life together that has been put on hold. Johnny's instinct to consider other means of fulfilment, alternative projects you might share, is a good one. Should you stay together, or take your chances elsewhere? Either way something you greatly value will be lost.' He shrugs his shoulders helplessly. 'It is a decision, I'm afraid, only you can make . . .'

With a leaden dread, I see our time is drawing to a close. 'Okay,' I mutter, blowing my nose, and wiping my eyes briskly.

'But I wish you well, Rose. Whatever you decide.'

I stumble to my feet, at a loss how to sign off. 'Thank you. Thank you for everything.'

'I'm sure I said this when we first met – my door is always open.'

Should I confess the true extent of the madness that has gripped me? I feel I must say something.

'I know this sounds ridiculous . . .' I hesitate, unsure quite how to proceed. 'I mean, I remember you warning me about this at the beginning. But I really was convinced you had celestial powers for a while.'

He smiles ruefully. 'Well, it's not only patients who labour under that delusion, I can assure you.

Embryologists suffering from a God-complex are an occupational hazard. Some of my students too . . .'

'And you?'

'Ahh, well . . .' His face takes on an expression of self-reproach. 'Regretfully, my human limitations are only too painfully evident to me, I'm afraid. As they are now to you.'

Outside his office, a news crew stand up eagerly when they see him, and he shakes my hand warmly, before turning to greet them. Downstairs in the lobby, I stand aside to make way for a patient who seems to pass me in a trance, as if drawn by an invisible leash up those chilly stairs. I step out onto the street, and the swing doors close slowly behind me for the last time.

On the way home I stop the car on a double yellow line, and walk out across the bridge. The little photograph spins sideways like a sycamore seed. A quick glimpse of hands as it tumbles. It flutters for some moments above a rusty barge, held fast on air currents, before the wind drops, causing it to plummet like a stone. Already it is no more than a speck, a scrap of flotsam and jetsam bobbing on the vast oily waters. Within seconds it is lost from view, on its way downstream to the sea.

10

My husband or a child. How was I to make such a choice? In the days and weeks that follow, I find a new thought stirring. We would never have a child that was biologically Johnny's. That much, I had to concede now, was undeniably the case. But we might still have a child.

Some time ago, in one of our early consultations, Dr Grisham had said that if ICSI didn't prove successful, we might consider the possibility of sperm donation. Donors remained anonymous, he had explained, and were chosen so that their colouring and build matched the husband's as closely as possible. Donor and husband's sperm would then be mixed before insemination, presumably to allow for a comforting margin of doubt if the procedure succeeded. At the time, Johnny had been adamant that he would never countenance such a prospect. And I too had discounted the notion out of hand, never really imagining, I suppose, that it would ever actually come to that. Now the time had come to reconsider.

Yet how would we ever explain to a child that we knew no more than the colouring and build of their genetic father? Wouldn't all three of us always wonder. For who *would* he be, this anonymous donor? A thoughtless medical student with a face full of angry blemishes wanting to earn a bit of easy money? Or a bespectacled bank clerk who derived some unsavoury thrill from the whole business. What kind of man *was it* that gave away his issue so casually, with no way of ever knowing if offspring had resulted, or of having any relationship with them if they had? Only a man with a heart of stone. I imagine his strange progeny playing obsessive computer games, unable to sustain eye contact or engage emotionally. And dimly I recall a fairytale that had haunted me as a child. It was the story of an elderly couple who found an abandoned baby on their doorstep. Filled with delight they had taken him in, nurturing him as their own, only to find, as the boy grew older, that he was a monstrous thing – a goblin child – who broke their hearts and destroyed their lives.

But if I can't countenance an anonymous donor, what possible solution can lead me forward now?

We sit, just the two of us, amidst the clatter of diners and swirl of hurrying waiters. An accomplished storyteller, Gabriel is regaling me with his latest setpiece. But the knot in my stomach makes it impossible to concentrate, the food before me as unpalatable as sawdust. How was it possible to be this nervous in the company of one of my oldest friends? We'd been at college together for three years. It was Gabriel I'd backpacked round India with that summer after I left. He talks amiably on, while I experiment quickly with opening lines, struggling to find something that sounds right. Impossible to remember now how this had ever seemed a good idea. It is some moments before I realise he is no longer talking, the silence snapping me to attention.

'You're miles away,' he says. 'What's up?'

So I tell him that we've just had our third IVF failure, and his expression gives way to the sympathetic and slightly uncomprehending one that always accompanied my attempts to update him on our progress. I explain we've finally realised that there was no point in putting ourselves through it anymore and he visibly brightens, nodding approvingly.

'Good for you . . . Good for you, Rose!'

'I'm afraid I've been feeling pathetically sorry for myself . . .'

'Oh, sweetheart . . .' He reaches out to take my hand. 'You're going to have *me* in tears in a minute.'

Though I thought I'd prepared a humorous line, close on my destination I can no longer recall it, my tongue rasping the top of my mouth like a pumice stone.

'So I've been doing a lot of thinking. As you do in these situations. And . . . This is going to sound very bizarre . . . But I just wondered whether . . .' I laugh shyly. 'Whether *you* would ever consider having a baby with me?'

Gabriel blinks once, then twice, in astonishment, and an incredulous sound like the honk of a sea lion bursts from his open mouth. Pushing his half-finished plate away, he reaches instead for a cigarette.

'Fucking hell, Rose!'

'We need a sperm donor, you see . . .'

'Right . . .' He lights the cigarette, and draws deeply on it before blowing a long plume of smoke at the ceiling, frowning. 'Nobody's ever asked me that before . . .'

We are unable to look one another in the eye, suddenly finding ourselves like a timid young couple on their first date.

'I'm sorry, Gabe. This must seem a bit out of nowhere.'

His aghast laugh confirms it. I've become so steeped in the language of reproduction, that it's only now, amongst the formal clink of silver cutlery on porcelain, that I see how outlandish the proposal must sound. The couple at the next table appear suspended mid-mouthful, waiting dumbstruck for Gabriel's reply, our eyes upon him as he flounders.

'Darling, I'm . . . honoured. Totally overwhelmed. But . . . Christ! I mean, why *me*? Why *my* child?'

I feel the next table's eyes swivel to me now, and lean forward, speaking as quietly as I can.

'Because you're a dear friend . . . with good genes . . . and . . . well, how else are you ever going to get a baby? All that gallivanting around with gorgeous young men is hardly going to produce a son and heir, is it?'

Gabriel's tendency to have his heart broken was an

ongoing source of debate between us. Over the years a series of beautiful youths had passed through his life. Each time he would pick himself up and dust himself down vowing he had at last learned his lesson. Yet though he longed for reciprocal love, he seemed fatally and unerringly drawn to the men least likely to offer it.

'I can't say I've ever lost sleep over it. I mean, it's never really crossed my mind ... A *child* ...' he says tentatively, trying the phrase experimentally.

'You don't have to give me an answer now ... I just want you to go away and think about it ...'

In the ensuing silence, seeing that the couple at the next table have at last resumed their desultory conversation, I add as a hasty afterthought: 'I mean, I'm not suggesting you have to sleep with me or anything.'

'No sex?' His relief is undisguised.

'No! No sex ...'

'Are we talking turkey baster here?'

'I don't know – I mean probably – I haven't really got that far ...'

Our laughter is brittle as we strain to regain our old ease in one another's company, and he drains his glass of wine greedily, before filling it again.

'So I'd just do the business, hand it over and that would be it?'

'That would be it. No nappy changing or homework duties of any kind.'

He nods thoughtfully.

'Oh God, Rose. I know how much this means to you.'

Though tears startle into my eyes, I shake my head, vainly attempting a light-hearted shrug. He pulls himself upright, pushing his shoulders back. Then he downs the wine in one again, before wiping his mouth quickly with the back of his hand, and planting the glass decisively. 'Okay then. You're on!'

'You will?' Shock then elation welling brightly at this sudden absolution. It was as if an apparently impenetrable obstruction has dissolved like tissue paper beneath my fingertips, and I'm light-headed with the simplicity of the solution. How had it taken me so long to find it? We clink our glasses together, laughing and shaking our heads. And I sit taking stock for a moment, still smiling and nodding, taking it all in.

'And Johnny? Obviously Johnny's cool about it all?'

'Well, to be honest, I haven't quite got that far . . . But I think he'll be fine. I'm sure he'll be fine . . .'

We both contemplate this for a moment.

'Why wouldn't he be fine?'

Gabriel sits back, and folds his arms gravely. 'Christ, Rosie. You've got some serious talking to do, old girl.'

'Well,' I manage a breeziness I don't entirely feel. 'I suppose that's the next bridge to cross.'

Outside on the street I embrace him, holding him close, overwhelmed with gratitude.

'Thank you,' I mutter into his collar.

'Not another word until you've talked to that man of yours,' he says sternly, before turning to go. I watch him as he walks away on unsteady feet, his breath streaming out in white clouds, and realise that I am still smiling and nodding. I watch him walk all the way to the end of the street before he turns the corner and vanishes. But still I stand, smiling and nodding, smiling and nodding.

As the traffic on the way home ebbs slowly along the Gray's Inn Road, my elation is already waning. Somehow I'm going to have to square this with Johnny, and I know perfectly well that it's going to be difficult. Know perfectly well, if I'm honest, what he'll say. When the consultant had raised the issue of sperm donation, he had been quite clear that he had no desire to raise another man's child. 'I want blood ties, continuation. *Our* child, Rose. Yours and mine. Not just *a* child. You do understand that, don't you?'

I imagine this theoretical child tossed between us on complex seas of unresolved resentment and guilt. Potentially a reproach to us both. What if the child resembled Gabriel? What if Gabriel developed strong paternal feelings towards the child? A decent, loving man, why would he not? It was difficult to believe both the marriage and the friendship could easily survive these lurking pitfalls unscathed. The feeling of a heavy weight pressing upon my shoulders has returned. Why did I have to agonise about everything in this way? These internal debates exhausting me, sabotaging every potential way forward.

The traffic before me is slowing as it joins the tailback at the lights. Green, amber, red.

And what would we tell the child? The truth would sideline Johnny. Yet a lie would deny the child their fundamental right to know its true origins. And anyway, there was always the danger that the truth might emerge after a blood test of some kind. I'd read about an American case like that only recently. A cherished child making the painful discovery that nothing was actually as it appeared. The whole plan was a time bomb. And yet the lure of a healthy gurgling baby now seems so tantalisingly close at hand. After all, this is no mere sentimental longing, I reflect indignantly. It is a *need*. A biological compulsion even. *'We are survival machines – robot vehicles programmed to preserve the selfish molecules known as genes.'* I'd come across the quote from Richard Dawkins just the other day, and the phrase had lingered potently in my mind. I was hard-wired to pursue this trajectory. I thought of Tamsin who had had three children, despite Pete's undisguised reluctance. Of my mother having three sons in pursuit of the daughter she longed for. There was an undeniable steel in women, an indomitable resolve to *achieve* life once the instinct was awakened. And if my biology is chasing genetic survival, isn't my heart just as surely pursuing the need to offer selfless love? To bring a child into the world, and nurture it through all setbacks, on into adulthood. And didn't needs create *rights*?

The lights hit green just at the moment a favourite song begins playing on the radio, instantly anaesthetising all worry. We'd work it out. Maybe Johnny would turn out to have had a change of heart since we last discussed the issue. So much else had changed.

These were not insuperable problems. He'd probably surprise me. Greet the proposal with open arms. Christ, we were so close to a breakthrough. No point in worrying about these things. You wouldn't even get out of bed in the morning if you thought too hard about it. Stop analysing. *Just do it*.

Amber. Red again. I ease the car to a halt once more.

A businessman is standing beside me at the lights, reading a document while he waits. As my car draws level with him, a sudden gust of wind snatches the paper from his hand. He is unusually tall, and as he hastens to retrieve it, his head and body roll on separate axes like a puppet. But just as his fingers are about to close round the paper, the wind whips it away again. Judging from his stricken face, the document is of great importance to him. Twice more he fruitlessly reaches out, and twice more the wind larkishly whips it just out of reach between the wheels of passing cars.

Then the lights are green again, and I'm borne forward on the flow of traffic once more. It is an omen. His fate will augur mine. I strain to catch a glimpse of his reflection, dreading to see him turn away in despair as the paper is shredded under the wheels of a passing lorry. The cars behind me are hooting as my foot idles at the accelerator, and I crane my head vainly at the mirror, the noise like pepper in my ears. Then he flashes back into view, gamely dodging between the treacherous lorries with their belching fumes, grimly determined. For the last time he stoops, and when he rises, I see he is triumphantly clasping the paper.

Catching the flash of my smile in the mirror, I speed the car forward, the ache inside me easing still further. Hope is warming my belly like a tiny blue pilot light. Everything was going to work out just fine.

I set down my coffee cup, the mail, and the morning's paper held at an awkward angle in an attempt to avoid smudges of print on my fingers. Johnny and I have arranged to talk over dinner this evening. When I sat down to join him for breakfast he had quite spontaneously double-taked, like someone in a children's show when a ghost appears beside them. I had explained it was important, that there were things we urgently needed to discuss and, somewhat hesitantly, he'd agreed. How oddly self-conscious we had been, sitting eating toast and sipping coffee together, sharing domesticity again just as in the old days.

I switch the computer on, its hum as it whirrs into action heralding the beginning of the working day, then click to receive e-mails. And here it is – gabrieldunmore@online.co.uk. I realise that subconsciously, since first waking, I've been suppressing the expectation of its inevitable arrival.

hang on, hang on. darling you are one of my oldest friends. you know i would cut off my right arm for you. but a baby! a baby would take me entirely out of my depth. think the wine must have gone to my head. let's not muddy the waters. sorry Rose. sorry.

Gabe

xxx

'I know you're probably angry with me right now. But, in the long run, in the long run, I promise you it's for the best.'

I had picked the phone up on a reflex, still reeling. Too late to regret it now.

'Are you?' Gabriel speaks tentatively into the silence.

'What?'

'Angry with me?'

'Of course not.'

He exhales despairingly. 'Oh God, you are. You're livid . . .'

'I think we're just going to have to ad lib this as we go. It's all a bit too modern to get my head round.' I hear my attempt at laughter falter into something that heralds tears.

'I've been up most of the night thinking about it, Rose. I wouldn't let you down lightly. I hope you know that.'

I glance at the time recorded on his e-mail entry, and there it is. 4.35 a.m. Now even those close to me were being drawn into the queasy moral morass. As if I carried some contagious contamination. A pang of compassion and shame assaults me.

'Oh Christ, I'm sorry, Gabriel.'

'I worry our friendship couldn't survive this. I worry about Johnny and what he'd feel. I worry about this child with two fathers. And the truth is, I've never been one of those gay men who secretly hankered after a child. I just haven't.'

'I understand. Honestly. Let's just forget it, shall we . . . move swiftly on.'

Yet a feeling of restraint is undeniably between us now, and perhaps hoping to overcome it, Gabriel's contrition moves by twists and turns to brotherly advice. He wonders whether I've ever considered adoption, and is undeterred when I explain we're too old. What about going to China or Romania? he persists. He tells me enthusiastically of all the couples he's read about who've successfully fought their way through the bureaucracy. But slowly increasing in volume, an urgent rift is beginning to thrum in my ears, making it harder and harder to concentrate.

My baby, my baby! Bone from my bone! Flesh from my flesh!

'I'll give it some thought,' I say coolly.

Gabriel, however, is warming to his theme; anxious to feel he has been able to offer some alternative kind of solace.

'I mean, there are so many different ways you could choose to look at this, aren't there?' he says thoughtfully.

'Are there?' The winter chill in my voice appears not to deter him.

'It's almost as if – and don't take this the wrong

way – but I couldn't help noticing how this baby thing distracted you from all your career frustrations. Don't you think there might be an element, a teeny-weeny element, of displacement going on here? Look at how you've set aside that photography book you were always going on about. And what's become of all those other projects you half pursued but never quite finished?'

Bone from my bone. Flesh from my flesh! Bone from my bone. Flesh from my flesh! Pulsing in my very waters, like the bass of one of those souped-up sound systems. Impossible to concentrate now.

'More and more women are choosing not to have children these days. Don't overlook the negatives, Rose. All those sleepless nights. The expense. The loss of freedom. And for what? In the end they only grow up and leave you right back where you started. I mean, maybe it's not the great answer to all life's shortcomings you've built it up to be. That's all I'm saying . . .'

From the soft nub of my fingertips, down to the horny curve of toenail, his words chafe and sting to the quick.

'Think about it. I mean, you were the last person I'd have expected to get so hung up on the whole baby thing. Darling, the old Rose would have cut her losses and –'

Claptrap, claptrap, hogwash, drivel! Claptrap, claptrap, hogwash, drivel!

The phone clattering from my bloodless grasp, the words snapped out, like white noise suddenly ceasing.

* * *

I no longer call friends or respond to their messages. The answering service gathers their voices and offers of activities, then I simply erase them, one by one. It's become a nightly ritual. Every day there are less and less. Even Gabriel's anxious voice is seldom to be found there now.

One evening I find only one message. I recognise Pete's voice instantly. He knows I've gone to ground, he says, but he just thought I'd like to know that Tamsin has had her baby. He sounds tentative, as if uncertain how I will receive the news. 'It was an emergency Caesarean, so they'll have to stay in hospital for a few days,' he continues. 'But they're fine.' His voice soaring despite himself. 'Mother and son both in fine fettle!'

I go straight away, heart flooding with emotion. Pausing only to buy flowers from the hospital gift shop, I take the lift to her ward, where the tropical heat greets me like a physical embrace. I stand scanning the rows of beds, until I see her at the far end. She's fast asleep, face pale, mouth pushed forward in a child-like pout. Her nightdress is open at the neck, the veins on her chest a network of blue, her breasts beneath the gauzy fabric swollen and heavy. And there beside her. My heart leaps. Her baby lies asleep in a clear Perspex bassinet. Like her, he is entirely abandoned to sleep, tiny fingers trailing a slow elegant arc through the air. He looks both ancient and new all at once, and I stand looking from one to another for a moment, amazed at their duality. I lay her flowers down amongst the bouquets that topple together on the side table, while the woman in the bed opposite sits nursing her own newborn baby, and smiling kindly upon us.

'I'll tell her you came by, shall I?' she says in an Irish accent.

'No, no. Don't worry . . . I'll call.' I step back overwhelmed, so many lactating women and babies on every side.

'He's a lovely little one, isn't he? A fine little man,' she says cosily, her eyes aglow. 'Though he's been terrible unsettled the last night. Still they're catching up now.'

I nod at her and step away. From somewhere down the long corridor comes the primal lowing of a woman in labour. Midwives at the desk confer urgently, then the matron hurries away towards the anguished cries, tights rubbing together with crisp purposefulness. I glimpse a lounge filled by mothers sitting with babies at their breast. Pass a pregnant woman in a nightie, moving with infinite heaviness, her great tummy thrust forward like the prow of a ship. Feather light, I whisk on and out. An electric energy has possessed me; a fizzing and crackling in my limbs, an urgency fluttering at my core.

Time to stop treading water. Got to get out there. Sort this thing out once and for all. *Yesterday is history, tomorrow is a mystery. Today,* the fortune cookie sweetness rings like a battle-cry down the years, *today is a gift* . . .

PART THREE

My father was the keeper of the Edison Light,
He married a mermaid one fine night,
And from this union there came three,
A porpoise and a porgy, and the other was me!

Yo ho ho, the winds blow free!
Oh for a life on the rolling sea!

Traditional maritime song

11

Can't say anything to anyone. If this plan's ever to work, no one must ever, even for a moment, suspect a thing. Doubt would be the canker in the heart of the rose. Doubt would be our undoing. Taking the magazine cutting from the secret place, I look carefully at it for the last time, then shred it into oblivion.

I arrive at the pub Pete and his cronies often hung out in just as the lunchtime rush is building momentum, steam from the open kitchen gathering in clouds above the heads of the hurrying cooks. It may be a long shot, but it's a start. Before me a humming gathering of energy-charged young people meet and greet one another, their talk and laughter filling the place with an exuberant din. I sit alone, scanning the faces, and though I order food too, it remains before me untouched, congealing. After an hour has passed and most people are eating, I know it's fruitless to remain. There's no one I recognise here, no connections to lead me further.

Then the fizzing and crackling is back, forcing me up from my seat. I go to the counter to pay my bill, restless to be gone, turning over my next move. As I wait my turn, I tap my impatience, keeping an eye on the mirror behind the bar for latecomers arriving through the door. Friends, acquaintances, my hungry eye roaming restlessly. Posters for plays are stuck on a column by the bar. A nice moody photograph for a new one at the Bush. A fuzz of text. Some quotes from critics. Some names. My eye slides away then back, one of the blurred faces calling to me, text cohering into instant pin sharp clarity. I'd found him. Bill Kelly. 8.00 p.m.

That night I am first to enter the tiny auditorium. The first to settle myself in the front row, savouring the scent of the theatre as I take my seat. At Bill's entrance every fibre of my being rises to attention. I watch his pacing, craning to hear the nuance of his line, my eye never leaving him even for a moment, the other actors moving like shadows about him. His athletic grace on the stage stirs a visceral charge that is all the confirmation I require. I scarcely listen to the meaning of his words, pay scant attention to the unfolding plot, straining only to intuit the thoughts that turn behind the actor's mask. Finally, at the curtain call, as he graciously dips his head at the patter of applause, I am up, stumbling over knees and feet, heading for the exit.

I have already checked where the stage door is, and stand with time in hand in the piss-smelling alley, the shrill wind like a knife at my throat. After a moment the cast begin to emerge one by one, calling farewells and jocular last taunts as they head their separate ways towards the bright lights of the high street. Then quick as a flash, he emerges too, stepping out from the gloom of the doorway. But I'm hard behind him as he hurries. No fear of him seeing me. Why would it ever cross his mind that he was being followed?

On we travel in fierce tandem, out of the dark night, down into the empty echoing bowels of the underground. There is scarcely a beat before the train is upon us. We sit opposite one another in the deafening clack of the carriage, he reading, my eyes upon him all the while. Here we are journeying abreast, so close I could lean forward and touch his knee. I won't speak to him, though. Even in my current fever, I know I risk destroying everything if my first approach is misjudged. If I strike a false note, if there is even a hint that I am on this crazed mission, we will never recover our step. Like a seasoned hunter I caution myself to bide my time, and step carefully.

He looks so beautiful as he reads, the downward sweep of his scanning eye, the peaceful cast of his sensual mouth. I anticipate in advance when he is getting off; am up before him, congratulating myself on my un-canny prescience as he rises too. And on we hurry once more, man and shadow. Out into the cold night again. Stalker and quarry. A savage elation soaring at our unacknowledged kinship as we hasten on in perfect step. We zigzag between streets, until he finally turns sharply. I hear the creak of the gate, then he is fumbling for his keys at the door of a small terraced house. His shoul-der twists as he struggles for a second with the lock, then the door flies open and swallows him. Caught plumply in his nest. I travel home with a song in my heart.

Things are going well. Very quickly I come to know the rhythms of Bill's day as though they were my own. He wakes late, long after Bo has taken their son to nursery. Has breakfast at a cafe on the corner, reading the *Guardian* from cover to cover, working backwards from the sports pages. Sometimes he drops into the bookies before meeting friends, often at the pub where I waited that seemingly fruitless lunchtime. My scrutiny holds him fast, binding him to me on silken threads. Once or twice we journey to an audition together.

As the days unfold, I even learn he is having an affair. She may be an actress too. I can only guess. But he meets her one day outside the restaurant she works in, and they embrace with passion, nuzzling hungrily at one another. This libidinous display only delights me, for now I can set aside the nagging worry that he might have reformed his philandering ways. I have chosen my prey well. There should be no delicate moral scruples to stay his hand when the moment comes.

But how to make the moment come? On this, I find myself perplexed. The days are spinning by. At night I scarcely sleep. Johnny thinks I'm immersed in new photographic projects and I let him believe. He appears relieved. Probably thinks I'm returning to my old self. That we are finding a way forward, that there can be a life together without children. But all the while I am watching and wondering, planning and plotting, a humming and thrumming pulsing ceaselessly in me now.

One day I come across the picture I took of Johnny as

we arrived at Xin Chao on the ferry. In that faraway time Before, when life had centred so lightly on its pivot. I'm touched by his youth, the rounded boyishness of his features – invisible at the time, and only defined now by absence. He looks boldly into my camera, a man poised to take life by the horns. It's a perfect day in the photograph, the sky and sea the colour of joy I remembered so well. There are people at the water's edge waiting to board the boat when it docks. One of them stands apart, watching our approach. It's the oddest thing, but I see now that the figure bears a remarkable resemblance to Bill. I smile in amusement, peering closer still. It seemed so unlikely. Yet the resemblance is undeniable. As we arrived could he really have been leaving? We must have unwittingly passed one another amongst the clamour of animals and people. The possibility makes me laugh out loud in frank astonishment.

And then it occurs to me one feverish, sleepless night, that I could get Bill's number and call on the pretext of wanting to photograph him for some non-existent magazine profile. At first I think of asking Tamsin for the number, but I'm wary of her acute eye, of her guessing something's afoot. So I resolve to swallow my pride and make things up with Gabriel. Which I do with such humility that he is instantly conciliatory too. We talk for just long enough that the fact that I want something from him doesn't undermine my gesture, and when I judge the moment to be right, as if on a casual afterthought, I ask for the number. And eager to consolidate our reconciliation, he not only gives me the number, but tells me that he's seeing Bill later and will mention it to him.

When I put the phone down I'm momentarily shocked at how ruthlessly I have engineered a dear friend into giving me what I need. It is as if the drive to procreate has become subverted into this elaborate stalking game, and I am only able to relate to people in terms of how much nearer they move me to my goal. A hollow self-loathing lacerates me. I have become a pitiable, desperate woman who will stop at nothing in pursuit of biological affirmation. But the thought of biological affirmation fires the lioness into life again. Back she comes prowling, undeterred, and seizing the phone I dial Bill's number.

His answer machine cuts me off mid breezy message. Days pass. Finally he calls. I miss him. I call him back. He's out again. Then he calls me back in the middle of a shoot. Though I'm photographing the new executive line-up of a merchant bank, I take the call immediately, leaving them looking awkwardly bemused in their formal rows at my hasty exit. I tell Bill we met once at one of Tamsin and Pete's parties, and though he claims to remember me, it's quite clear he doesn't. I spin him a garbled story about a piece I am doing, a line-up of new faces, a 'who to watch' Sunday supplement thing. And he agrees in an offhand, don't think I'm flattered, but I'll do you a favour kind of way, and we arrange a date a month hence. I have done my calculations in advance. In addition to being Hanukkah and the first day of winter, it is also ovulation day in my diary.

Then, muttering profuse and cheerful apologies, I return to the executive board, now irritably checking their watches. So it's not until the evening, when I've dropped the rolls of film off at the lab and I'm on my way home, that I have a chance to feel sudden fear and trepidation about what the hell I've got myself into.

For what exactly am I going to do with him? How does a photo shoot segue into a seduction? I realise I've been assuming that somehow his legendary instincts as a philanderer are going to smooth the way. The sudden lurching thought of Johnny throws me still further. And hard on its heels, the flavour of contemptible desperate person is rank in my mouth again. It occurs to me that the only way I'm going to make this work is to keep the image of a prowling lioness firmly at the forefront of my mind. For though I've never in my life made a move on a man, I feel confident that the lioness will know how. And when I remember my goal, and recall how long this goal has thwarted me, the flame of righteous indignation ignites so fiercely that I am fired straight back into action. *My baby, my baby! Bone from my bone! Flesh from my flesh!*

In a flash of inspiration I recall an artist's studio in Shoreditch. An airy gabled space, with a platformed bedroom in the eaves. It belonged to an artist, Sharon Branson, who I'd once been commissioned to photograph. I remember reading that she was away working in South America. So I call her gallery, who call her, and successfully negotiate to rent it for a day. The fee is astronomical. But I don't care. Our debts are so immense now, it's just another nought on a credit card bill. All obstacles are tumbling before my war march. I understand for the first time the true power of positive thinking. And it strikes me how extraordinarily simple and self-evident the right solution was, once you finally stumbled upon it. There it had been unrecognised all this long while, the way forward, the only way. Not just for me, but for Johnny as well.

In the intervening weeks I am newly tender to him. If this worked, Bill and Johnny's close resemblance in colouring meant he need never suspect a thing. Indeed it dawns on me with revelatory insight, that this resemblance, together with their mutual intelligence and creativity, merely demonstrated that my plan to get one man's DNA to substitute for the other was no more than a mere technicality. No more than pollination. I see clearly now that my physical attraction to both men was simply an instinctive recognition of this fact. Any resulting child would be in every way Johnny's. And in protecting him from the truth I was merely opening up the possibility of an untroubled fatherly love, which would otherwise be forever denied him. It was his stubbornness on the issue that forced my hand, and gave me no option but to pursue this clandestine plan. There had been many times over the years when he had saved me from myself. Now it was my turn to save him. It was the best possible solution for us both. Far from being an act of betrayal, I think, this was my gesture of conciliation. Of love. It was quite extraordinary how often these apparent moral absolutes were so often simply a matter of perspective.

I recall my former concern about a blood test one day revealing a doubt over the child's paternity, and dismiss it instantly now as absurd. In the unlikely event that such a situation were to arise, the overlap would be so close, there would be no disparity to uncover. But it is on the most potentially hazardous pitfall, that I find myself most supremely confident of all. Johnny would never wonder how I had become pregnant when his sperm count was so low. Far more than I, he had always treasured those stories of conceptions that occur against all odds. Had always clung to the hope that fate might grant us a fluky reprieve too. It moved me beyond words to think I was finally about to bestow the longed-for miracle, to free him at last from the tyranny of disappointment and self-castigation.

And what of Bill? I give the morality of robbing Bill in this way only glancing consideration. For it struck me that his years of philandering indicated a certain callowness of spirit that forfeited the right to delicate scruples. I give more serious consideration, however, to whether he might connect my pregnancy to our encounter and claim paternity. But then our lives overlapped so little; the evening would quickly become lost in the mists of time. By the time he heard – *if* he ever heard – I couldn't in truth see him sitting down with a diary to calculate. And anyway, if he were ever to make the connection, a paternity claim would mean a public confession. And from all I knew about him, he was a man who had far too much to lose. To pursue a future with the glamorous Bo, he would have no option but to keep his own counsel.

Above all, it was the straightforwardness of the encounter that reassured me. To Bill, I would be just another casual lay. If our encounter weren't successful first time, I would simply pursue the liaison until it was. Then walk away without a backward glance.

Inside me blazes fire. I feel the scorch of its flash in my eyes, the ferocity of its combustion in my loins. For tonight is the night I take control; finally stop being blown by the winds of fortune, at long last slip the frigid embrace of medical science.

I pick up the keys and let myself into the studio first thing that morning. Though our meeting is not until early evening, I light the industrial heaters, change the sheets on the bed and choose some music. It's only then that I remember, somewhat belatedly, to set up the portrait studio. A white backdrop. The portable lights. Even though it's a sham, I'm thinking Richard Avedon. And who knows. It might be nice to send him the photographs. The night he so unwittingly closed the circle.

Bill arrives on time, but I see at once he's distracted. I offer him a glass of wine, and he takes it absently, appearing scarcely to notice it in his hand. He throws aside his leather jacket, and glances briefly around the airy studio. 'Great pad,' he says, pulling up a battered chair and beginning to roll a joint. 'Is it yours?'

'No, it belongs to a friend. I just rent it sometimes. Pretend I'm one of the happening young artists hanging out in Shoreditch for a little while . . .'

He smiles a quick dismissive smile. 'Actually, I think you'll find Peckham's the new Shoreditch.'

'I'll take your word for it.' I'm fiddling with lights, hoping to appear a little professionally distracted. In fact his physical proximity is making me jumpy, a flutter of fear in my belly now he's actually before me. I watch him surreptitiously as he rolls and twists the joint into shape, a lovely dexterity as he cranes gracefully towards his work like a watchmaker. His insouciance evokes a familiar pang in me, reminding me of that grainy photograph.

'You've got a little boy, haven't you?'

'That's right. Noah. Cussed little blighter. Drives everyone mad. Takes after me his mother says . . .' He looks at me directly for the first time, rolling the joint carefully between thumb and forefinger. 'So what d'you want me to do then?'

'Well, it's just a simple portrait shot really. Head and shoulders. Black and white . . .'

He surveys the backdrop and lights, frowning.

'Fuck. I hate having my photograph taken. Always thought the Africans were on to something with their theories about stealing the soul.'

The mention of stealing makes me blanch guiltily. A sensation that metamorphoses almost instantly into savage joy. We are on our way. It seems extraordinary to have got so far.

'It's entirely painless, I promise you.'

I touch his arm.

'Trust me,' I say airily. And he laughs with genuine amusement. 'You've probably been traumatised by too many encounters with paparazzi.'

'Probably.'

'Let's give it a whirl.'

He sits down on the studio stool and I turn the music up. It feels convincing. Even to me it feels real now.

'Just face me head on.'

I reach out and touch his face gently, indicating his eye line. Behind the camera I am safe, invisible. I'll take a roll, then think about making a move. Momentarily the reticent Rose stirs within me. A flutter of trepidation. But I concentrate on the image through the lens. His finely formed mouth. The luminous penetration of his eyes. He poses for a few frames, visibly restless in the glare of lights.

'Listen, d'you mind if I have a puff of this? If we just take a break for a minute . . .' He holds the joint up plaintively.

'Not at all.'

He lights it and takes a deep inhalation.

'We're rehearsing this new play at the Cottesloe. And between you and me, things are not going exactly brilliantly. Only a week to first preview, and my character's dying on his feet. I have this horrible feeling of impending doom.' He waves away the smoke that's drifting into his eyes. 'Cutting-edge director from the fringe. Face full of piercings and not a fucking clue. Almost rang to say we'd have to reschedule.'

He inhales again, holding the smoke down, savouring its effects.

'I go to bed totally wiped out. Then I just lie there tossing and turning ... half-cocked rewrites buzzing round my head ...'

I'm resting my arm on the tripod ready to resume. But I see that a frank exchange would be good. Could conjure quick intimacy.

'Christ,' I say, smiling candidly. 'You sound just like me. You're talking to one of the world's great experts in insomnia.'

His laughter rewards me, and emboldened I strike out again.

'Maybe the two of us should set up a late night support line ...'

He hands me the joint, visibly relaxing as he exhales. 'You strike me as rather a calm person.'

'Do I?' I fill my lungs conspicuously in a gesture of comradely complicity. 'Well, so do you come to that. But isn't that what they call the "swan syndrome"? All outwardly serene, but paddling like mad beneath the surface.'

He smiles, his teeth strikingly white and even. And somewhere behind those eyes a predatory wolfish glint fires, his gaze sweeping me appraisingly, snagging fleetingly on my wedding ring, which I see too late now I should have removed.

'Aren't swans famously monogamous?' The query in his tone is lightly teasing, but lost for a suitably flirtatious riposte, I make do instead with a coquettishly evasive smile. At this the glint in his eye hardens into resolve. The moment to make a move close at hand now, my breath coming in soft footfalls. He takes my wrist, drawing me with him to the sofa, throwing himself down. With what effortless practise he takes matters into his hands I marvel, falling so close beside him our knees momentarily brush.

'Didn't you spend some time in Vietnam?'

Somewhere, I remember, I have the photograph to show him. He nods, his eyes locked unambiguously now on mine.

'Because I think we may just have missed each other there. Stayed on this incredible island . . .' I wave a distracted hand, disconcerted to discover I'm already too stoned to remember its name. Then, 'Xin Chao!' we both say in unison, and laugh in shared amusement. I fill my lungs with smoke again, its benediction eddying through my limbs, as he reaches gently to brush a tendril of hair from my face.

Who would have thought it would go so well, so easily? is my last coherent thought before an overpowering wave of jittery paranoia strikes me a glancing blow, signalled by a hallucinatory rush as the room shifts on its axis and a nauseous faintness sings ethereally at my ear. Dimly I make out the staccato voice of survival muttering low through the dizziness.

Find bathroom . . . lock door . . . wait till head clears . . .

I lay down on the cold concrete floor of the ramshackle bathroom. Pull yourself together. Get a grip. Get a grip. And hard on the heels of the mantra, regret. Bitter regret. What had possessed me to take the damn thing, to smoke so much, so greedily? I rise experimentally to my feet, but another wave of giddiness instantly overcomes me, and I wrestle open the casement window and lean out, sucking in cool air like a fish. Bill is sitting below me on the fire escape, benignly observing the glittering skyline of the city. He looks up, smiling amiably.

'Won first prize in the Amsterdam dope festival!' he calls, raising the last of the joint in one hand. 'I tell you. Hits the spot every time.' I manage a nod, before slipping from view.

After a while I hear he has put on music. Something indolently bluesy curls through the night. Perhaps even now he is dimming the lights and undressing. I turn for the door one more time, staggering sideways, valiant to the end. The shower curtain evaporates beneath my grip and tripping over the ledge, I find myself propelled headlong into the shower, falling with a clatter of shampoo bottles, and knocking the showerhead, which baptises me momentarily in spangled water. Though the water somewhat revives me, much of my hair is now sodden. It occurs to me dimly that if my situation didn't feel so perilous, it might be amusing. Might still become so with the passage of time. But right now. Right now, I am out of my depth.

The paranoia is making my teeth chatter. I have been in here for what feels a very long time. He will be wondering what has become of me. Too polite to bang on the door, he will presumably assume I have been felled by some terrible gastric crisis. How was I ever going to emerge from here as the slinky femme fatale the evening required? I attempt to apply lipstick, but the line of my mouth proves strangely elusive. I appeared to have added a new curve to the cupid's bow. No matter. Though the hair was undeniably dripping like melting wax across one shoulder. Stupefied hollows in a gargoyle's face, my eyes goggle back at me.

It comes to me that a humorous line might smooth my re-entrance and provide the glue to mend the un-ravelling momentum. Though I can't think what the line might be, I know it is going to come to me in the airy space that lies beyond this cramped enclosure. Think lioness. I throw open the door with fierce concentration. Bill is rifling through Sharon's CD collection.

'Hmmm. Definitely idiosyncratic,' he says without looking up. 'Francoise Hardy or Bonny Prince Billy?'

My mouth is dry, language skittering away from me still. If I can just regain the camera, we'll be back on track. And since no humorous line is coming to me, I smile instead. Smiling lioness. Bill glances up.

'Christ!' he says. 'Are you all right?'

What could he mean? The paranoia returns with a ferocious shout. I gesture at the makeshift backdrop, inviting him with a brave attempt at vivacious laughter, to join me there. But the walk across the room is strangely complex. I alternately walk on giant flippers, or in adjusting my gait, don the wooden stride of a third-rate television presenter straining for spontaneity. Somewhere centre stage, as if momentarily possessed by Tourette's syndrome, I dance with nimble gaiety around an obstacle of some kind. At least I fear I have. Though close action replay reveals it to be quite possibly just another unsubstantiated paranoia.

Bill is frowning, watching me intently. It comes to me with a terrible clarity that he evidently knows exactly why I have brought him here, and sees the whole thing for the hollow masquerade and sham it really has been. That he is even now regarding me with scornful contempt. How had I made my intentions so transparent? My heart is pounding in my chest now, humiliation claggy in my throat. Perhaps in the first rush of chemicals through the bloodstream, a confession of some kind burst unbidden from my mouth.

'What the bloody hell's happened to your hair?' he says.

'I know. It's ridiculous, isn't it? I've been dancing a fandango with the shower . . .' I hear myself laugh girlishly. A strange affected laugh I have never heard before. But at least I seem to have regained the power of speech. It was going to be all right. Bill has returned to his seat in the makeshift studio, the lights making his face vivid once more. Now, however, the camera feels curiously unstable in my grasp, the parts moving alarmingly, like a Rubik's cube. *Just play for time*, a voice urges me. *Play for time*, it says again out of the corner of its mouth, like a cartoon gangster. 'Look,' I hear myself say. 'I'm just going to check whether Sharon's got a spare light meter lying around somewhere . . .'

I open the store cupboard, and step inside. And find myself inexplicably on the landing, cavernous stairs before me. Too late it dawns on me. I have chosen the wrong door. And now it is perfectly clear. No choice but to keep on going. As I descend the stairs, the waves of paranoia begin at last to fall away, clattering behind me on the linoleum treads.

Out on the street, the cold air sends a shot of sobriety through my system. *Just keep on going,* I think, walking as fast as I can now. Don't look back. Wipe the whole sorry business from your mind.

12

When my eyes snap open, I find I am lying in darkness, and that a crystal clarity now frames my thoughts. I've barely taken in the quiet breath of Johnny sleeping beside me when the memory of the past evening roars out of the gloom, as luridly loud and highly coloured as a pantomime. I lie very still, attempting to make some kind of sense of it all.

I see that in the past few weeks a kind of madness has overtaken me. I close my eyes again, listening for a moment to Johnny's tranquil breathing and wonder whether I should wake him and beg forgiveness. What could I have been thinking of? I sit up to look at him. Touchingly vulnerable in sleep, and yet entirely removed from me. No idea what strange plans I have been hatching. Our lives have become parallel ones, nothing connecting them any longer.

I get up and walk round the house, the shadows like thick felt. Seeking company, I switch the television on and flick channels in a desultory manner. I watch an Open University broadcast for a moment, though the words of the bearded man who stares out at me are so dryly academic they seem scarcely English. The

sensation of heavy shadows pressing in is countered unexpectedly by a vertiginous agoraphobia. I am spiralling,
plummeting like that little photograph as it fell towards
the water. And I'm overwhelmed by how I will contain
this intensity of aloneness. I try to think of friends I could
call. But just like Johnny, they are all sleeping deep,
untroubled sleeps. How can I contaminate them with
my troubles? I pick up the phone and call directory
enquiries, and they give me the number of the Samaritans so matter-of-factly I might be asking for the Gas
Board. And as I dial the number I know that I have drifted
beyond the containment of my habitual world. Far, far
away, the people I loved slept soundly, while I was borne
out into the night without end.

'Hello, Samaritans. How can I help?'

How had it come to this?

'I'm here. Just take your time . . .'

I put the phone down softly. Don't want it to sound
like an angry slam. I think of the Samaritans man sitting
in a dingy office above a shop somewhere. Having pulled
the short straw and got the graveyard shift. The felt is
stifling my nostrils, like a fur ball in my throat.

I start the car as softly as I can. It feels important to
make as little impact as possible on the world. I illumi-
nate the road with the sidelights only and switch the
radio on, but so low I can scarcely hear it. Then I slide
the car out onto the wet road, drawn by a longing for an
empty highway where sheer speed alone might numb
my aching heart.

London falling away behind me, diminishing all the

time in my rear-view mirror. The trees and houses on either side are stark silhouettes against the drab sky. And all that fills my mind now is the white lines flashing towards me, the pulse of the tarmac beneath my wheels and the ebb and flow of speed as I change lane, once or twice, the dull thud of Catseyes requiring me to sharply adjust my trajectory.

At length, the road plunges through ancient forest, the car's headlamps bouncing starkly off the trunks of the skeletal trees that appear to come leaping out of the dark beyond. As I pull up at the side of the house, the road is awash with a thousand tiny rivers, filling the air with the mushroom smell of sodden earth. The absence of any car outside assures me Tamsin and Pete can't be here. I had no idea this was where I was headed, but now I'm here I can imagine no other destination. The mud clutches greedily at my shoes as I step out into the snap of early morning air. The familiar waft of diesel fuel from the old garage marks my entrance as I open the garden gate, and I slide my hand along the door jamb until I find the cold metal of the key sweetly hidden there. The clapboard wood of the house is dark and swollen with saturated moisture, water dripping from the eaves and running gurgling through the guttering pipes.

The clunk of the key in the latch is reassuringly familiar. Now the embrace of the kitchen, an exhalation of warm breath from the Aga turned low. The silence in the house beyond is a deep and abiding hush. Tamsin and Pete's new baby would keep them away from their cottage for a few weeks more. Now the embrace of the sitting room. I make no impact upon its peacefulness. No more than a current of air moving through. Dark rafters high above my head, and the skylights streaked by the tears of rain. I walk my ritual arrival walk. Spin the zoetrope that makes the little juggler appear to catch the balls. Read the dusty invitations along the mantelpiece. But I'm careful not to move anything from its place. No more than a pair of disembodied eyes.

Walking as softly as I can, I examine the black-and-white photographs that are propped everywhere, each an old friend. Tamsin staring pensively out of the kitchen window, her first baby slumped asleep on her shoulder. A New Year's Eve party, with the guests blurred like ghosts. Her second child at six months looking wide-eyed into the camera. Johnny and I, arm in arm, smiling broadly.

Outside a grey day glimmers dully now. I borrow a coat and scarf from the rack, and step out into the lane. A woman is riding down the road towards me, her horse snorting little plumed clouds. For a moment I fear she will greet me and break the spell, but she looks blindly away down the long lane. As they pass, the great stench of warm animal is florid in my nostrils, the horse's huge thigh muscles bulbous with vitality, and the timbre of its heels thunderous castanets. Though as they pass away behind me, the sound fades almost instantly to a melancholy hollow clack. I walk on, invisibility making me weightless, and turn off into the forest, beech leaves slippery underfoot. And as the ground falls steeply, the arching boughs of the ancient trees almost instantly screen me on every side. Rivulets of water cascade from mossy banks, secret well springs bursting irrepressibly. Occasionally through the trees a glimpse of distant half-flooded meadows, reflecting the grey arc of sky. Inner and outer have merged entirely. I am bleak, barren. I am winter.

I walk and walk, time here suspended. Sometimes I lose my footing and slip. The mud has come to the top of my boots and saturated my trousers, and presently the sensation of cold becomes so insistent I start to come to. Words now finally forming as consciousness awakens. This has to end. This half-life. This waiting. I see that now. Our lives have been suspended for too long. It's time to let go. If I am to stay with Johnny, there will be no baby. There will be no inheritance. We are the end of a line. An evolutionary full-stop. And I sit down amongst the sighing of trees and weep for the flow of life that runs dry in me.

There are scratchings and scutterings beneath the floorboards, and at night the heavy feet of creatures in the rafters. Cold draughts pass mysteriously to and fro like internal weather fronts, and sometimes when the rain has fallen all afternoon without relief, the house groans and shifts in its foundations. Wrapped in old blankets, I rifle through the teetering tins in the kitchen cupboard, and plunder the iced-up freezer. In a rickety sideboard I come across dusty bottles of long forgotten liqueurs, which I sip experimentally from an eggcup to ease my melancholy spirits.

I make no plans other than to unplug the phone, and very quickly day merges into night, the daylight hours so short, that when I wake I discover I've entirely missed them. The first day bleeds into a second, the second into a third. Mainly I concentrate on keeping the fire burning. For as long as there is a low flame in the hearth, I can lie dozing in its halo of warmth. Contained in the embrace of the waterlogged forest, I feel suspended from my troubles, a numbness keeping me steadfast. Though increasingly in the twilight world between sleep and wakefulness, I find the same unresolved question. That if I were to stay with Johnny, could I find a way to make our life, with all its unfulfilled longing, suffice?

On the third day I awake with a start to find Tamsin standing before me.

'*Christ!*' she is exclaiming. 'Christ, Rose!' She surveys the wreckage of the room around me. 'Are you okay?'

I nod stupidly, disorientated by sleep, confused at her distressed urgency. She says the cleaner had called her, announcing she'd found a dishevelled woman asleep in front of the fire. So she'd come immediately. She runs a hand through her unbrushed hair.

'What were you thinking of?' she shouts, beside herself

with exasperation now she has established I'm at least alive. 'Johnny's been going crazy, imagining all kinds of terrible fates that might have befallen you. The police have put you on the Missing Person's Register . . .' She trails away, words failing her. There are smudges of baby milk on her dark shirt, and she holds the car keys in one hand, with the baby dangling from a car seat in the other. 'Didn't it occur to you people would be worried? Just one quick phone call was all it would have taken.'

After so long in silence, her sudden appearance and the tirade of words is overwhelming. I pull myself slowly upright, rubbing my eyes, uncertain with the curtains closed, whether it was day or night.

'I mean, I had no idea, *no idea* that you were going through all that IVF stuff again. Do you think I'm a bloody mind-reader or something?' A flush of red has crept across her neck, her face oddly swollen. Then she bursts into tears, plonks the baby's car seat on the floor, and embraces me fiercely. 'You have to sort yourself out, Rose,' she says, as I rest a dazed head against her shoulder. 'Enough is enough.'

She stands up briskly again, and begins gathering up the half-finished tins of food that encircle me, emptying the scattered debris into a bin liner, before dragging the stained duvet and pillows back to her bedroom. I retire to a chair while she works, and the baby and I sit observing one another with blank expressions of mutual stupefaction.

*   *   *

217

I watch the dreary winter landscape slide past the car window, the flat scrubby fields giving way at length to the industrial estates that fringed the city. It's a relief to be swept up like this, comforting to hear the rise and fall of changing gears, Tamsin's strong hands upon the wheel. Johnny meets us on the pavement outside our flat, and I'm shocked at his bloodless countenance.

'You've lost weight,' he says flatly. Tamsin has vanished from my side. I turn in time to see the car pulling away, her pinched face averted from the dismal spectacle the two of us must present.

We stand facing one another and I think of how I might throw my arms around him. '*I'm sorry,*' I would say quietly, and perhaps despite himself, the rigidity in his body would soften against mine. '*I'm so sorry,*' I would say again, my tears dropping onto the warm crook of his neck. '*It's you I want. Nothing else matters.*' I imagine his assenting nod, his knees seeming to buckle slightly. '*Come on you,*' he'd say gruffly, taking my hand and turning towards our front door.

Instead we stand stiffly aghast.

'I'll be at Mark's,' he says in a tight voice, and holds out the door key. 'Here. You'll need this.'

I clench its metallic coldness so tightly it burns the skin of my palm. 'Okay,' I'm nodding my head vigorously, in shock, yet anxious to seem reasonable. 'Okay.'

We both start to talk at once, then falter, than start again, our bodies jerking anxiously, all synchronicity now so entirely lost between us we are like tin cans clattering together.

'I'll call you,' he says, stepping backwards. 'When I'm ready. When you're ready. See where we are . . .'

13

Bleak winter gives way to the promise of spring. Then spring to the lush fullness of summer. A compassionate lady from Relate presides over our agonised and lengthy negotiations. And somewhere in that long cold spring we agree tentatively to try living together again. Then, as the days warm and lengthen, to accept an invitation to join Tamsin and Pete with their three children in Ibiza.

As we leave the airport, heading northwards in the hire car, with the map propped before us, we recall other journeys we have made, and the various adventures that had occurred on them over the years. The old travel camaraderie lends an easy conviviality, and we laugh at the memory of the time we feared we might be stranded forever on Xin Chao.

'I've always wondered,' I say teasingly. 'Did you *really* forget you'd left all those documents in that bag – or had you actually hidden them there?'

Johnny turns with genuine astonishment.

'What kind of question is *that*?' he asks so indignantly that I hasten to amend my words, not wanting things to sour between us.

'Well, sometimes these things can be more *subconscious* than concious . . .'

'*Did I subconsciously set out to create a situation* in which we would be stranded in the middle of nowhere together?' His indignant tone, descends the octaves, until the words slow reflectively, and he falls silent, seeming despite himself, to be struck by the idea. 'Maybe. Yeah. Maybe I did,' he says thoughtfully, after a moment or two. 'It never occurred to me before.' He swivels his head back to the road, looking so startled that we laugh in unison again. How absurd it was that you could know something, and yet keep it from yourself. He shakes his head wonderingly. 'Maybe I did . . .'

Very soon the houses that line the road give way to almond and olive groves. Feathery fronds of wild fennel thrust up from the hedgerows, and every now and then a pink or orange shock of oleander. At length the road rises up to cross the mountains, quick glimpses of sea flashing between the pine trees, and eventually, rounding a corner, we catch the first glimpse of Tamsin and Pete's rented villa, with its distinctive castellated tower, high on the mountain side above us.

In the searing heat of August, formless days unfold indolently before us, hour upon hour spent lying prostrate, immersed in a book, dazzled by the vast blue dome of sky. Very quickly the four of us fall into an easy routine, taking it in turns to cook, lingering leisurely over chaotic meals on the terrace. Tamsin's baby sleeps for hours at a time, his cheeks flushed in the heat, while Lily and I sometimes sit together, drawing pictures or singing songs I am surprised to find have lain dormant since I was a child myself.

Johnny sets himself the task of teaching Will to swim, occasionally calling us to come and admire his pupil's gratifying progress. As city pallor recedes, our skins grow golden under the sun, and a sensual self-regard steals over us. Freed now from the pressure to check charts and perform, a healing grows steadily in the heat of the day, flowering like night-stock in the balminess of the evenings. Each night the moon swells rounder and more luminous in the night sky, and once or twice from across the valley, we catch the feverish thunder of distant drums.

One morning we pack a picnic and set off over the brow of the hill, following the old stone track through the pine trees. Our pace is slow, the children stopping often to examine the pine cones and snail shells that litter the path. Looking after them required a kind of submitting, I could see that. Each moment of their day was entirely independent of any thought beyond the moment itself. Tamsin and I soon fell behind, taking it in turns to coax them on as they dawdled. We could hear Johnny and Pete just ahead, animatedly discussing Johnny's plan to sail around the world. They were capping each other with places that must be visited, and sights that must be seen. 'Why don't we all go together?' Pete was saying. 'Just seize the moment – while the children are still young enough. Take a crash course in sailing, pool resources, put all our jobs on hold for a year!' They are immersed, conspiring in the fantasy of how life might be otherwise, just as they so often used to in the days Before.

'Christ, can you imagine. A whole year. All of us stuck on a tiny boat?' Tamsin grimaces. 'Who d'you think would crack first?'

I smile, relieved at how the alarming craziness of the plan seems defused by her mockery, and swing my arms airily. 'Let them dream.'

Over the top of the spur, a man comes strolling with four dogs wheeling at his feet. He stops and watches our approach as we struggle up the gathering incline, frequently pausing now to carry one or the other of the children as they flagged.

'Lost?' he says, when eventually we draw level. We stand wiping our foreheads, catching our breath.

'No, no. Just exploring.'

He has a wizened face, as if the sun has sucked all the succulence out, leaving just a papery leather covering to lie across the bones. About his neck hang a complex array of beads and amulets.

'Keep walking, and you'll come to Tanit's cave,' he says, shielding his eyes against the sun. He points. 'Bear left off the track there. It's just a few minutes through the trees. Come. I'll show you.' The children are animated again, excited at the prospect of a cave. Would it have dragons Will wanted to know? Or lions? 'Tanit was the goddess of love, death and fertility.' The man walks authoratively, a little ahead of us, as if appointing himself our guide. The Carthaginians had first brought her to the island and dedicated the cave to her, he went on.

Though sadly there wasn't much to see anymore, most of the contents preserved in the archaeological museum in Ibiza town.

Now the sea opens up before us, and we find ourselves beside a rocky overhang. In the shade, by squinting our eyes, we can just make out the dark mouth of the cave. The man leads the way, Johnny and Pete following close behind, all three quickly swallowed up in the gloom. But the children and dogs instinctively hang back, fearful of the gaping hole. First Will, then Lily, take it in turns to hoot timidly, before bolting back to Tamsin and me.

We sit down in the shade close by, and begin unpacking the picnic, while Lily twines about me as I work.

'Is this okay?' Tamsin asks unexpectedly, so studiedly offhand I shake my head puzzled.

'How do you mean?'

'You know. For you two. Being around the kids all the . . .' She trails away delicately, and begins to slice chorizo into carefully precise segments. Poor Tamsin. Feeling she must walk on eggshells. What had I done to my friends?

Did I mind? I consider for a moment, and am surprised by what I find. 'Sometimes a wistful kind of pang ambushes you. But mostly . . . mostly I can honestly say it's been the greatest of pleasures.'

She scours my face before finally nodding, apparently satisfied. 'Good,' she says approvingly. 'That's good.'

'Did you think I was a lost cause?'

She hesitates, before smiling with an unexpected candour. 'For a while,' she nods. 'Yes. I think I did.'

The men soon reappear, all three blinking and squinting in the sunlight. They had found half-burnt candles in the cave, together with recent gifts of coins and little hand-written notes.

'Looks like Tanit worship is alive and well then,' Pete says, rubbing his hands in satisfaction, as if they were intrepid archaeologists returning from a challenging field trip. Our guide accepts our offer of lunch, falling greedily upon the meal spread out before us. His name was Arnie, he said, between mouthfuls, and he lived close by, making a living selling dope in the bars and clubs along the south coast. Born in Canada, he had lived an itinerant and precarious life.

'I've always let the winds of fortune be my guide,' he explains, chewing noisily. 'Criss-crossed the world a few times. Found myself getting off the ferry in Ibiza town one day with only ten dollars in my pocket. Hitchhiked across the island, and somehow shipped up here.'

We sit for some time, passing food and drink to and fro, reflecting on the places we have been, and the places yet to see, while the shadows begin to lengthen and cicada's shriek in the afternoon heat.

Just as we are beginning to pack up, a volley of hoots sound from the track below, and the lolling dogs leap instantly to their feet, barking agitatedly. Arnie stumbles up, hushing them, brushing the crumbs from his lap. 'My carriage awaits me!'

We stroll with him down the track. A battered pick-up truck sits ticking in the heat, a sulky-looking woman leaning with folded arms in the driver's seat. Though she is dressed in a sari, and wears a bindi on her forehead, she looks more German than Asian. Tamsin and I nod and smile at her, but she makes no attempt to reciprocate. The dogs clamber up into the open back, and Arnie has barely taken his seat beside her before she has angrily crunched the car into gear and shot off down the track, kicking up a cloud of dust on the parched earth.

L ate one afternoon I take a walk, following the road's downward curve, striking off at random along an unmarked turning. The path turns and turns upon itself in sharp descending corkscrews, each new vista through the trees different from the last. First dense pine trees, then a house half hidden, its shutters barred. Further down now a vast ashy sweep of burnt rock face where a forest fire must have swept through. Though close up, I see that wispy saplings are regenerating, springing up again from the torched earth. I keep walking, walking down into the lee of the mountain.

Here and there, monolithic cauliflower heads of stone remain exposed amongst the dense forest scrub, their exuberant upward thrust perfectly freezing in time the explosive moment of energy when the earth's plates once sheared upwards to form these mountains, cleaving the deep fissure of valley between. Pine trees cluster closer and closer, the light falling sharply away as I descend. An uneasiness creeps upon me. Down and down the path sinks. Down and down I go into the murky twilight.

At last I hear the sea. And passing through the arching bows of giant bamboo, like the curtains of a theatre, I find myself upon a small pebbly beach. It's calm tonight, the sea rustling peacefully against the stony incline. I walk stumbling across the pebbles and pause beside it, hot and tired from the long descent.

I'm disconcerted to find I'm not alone. A young couple stand at the far end of the cove, immersed in agitated conversation. They look like locals. She gesticulates angrily, while he leans his weight against a fishing boat. He bends so low, his forehead is resting on his hands. Perhaps he is weeping. Perhaps she is breaking off their affair. I see the agony in his stoop, as if he is literally being felled by her words. Then he reaches out to touch the paintwork of the boat. And on the instant, I see he is in actual fact just a fisherman who has come to check his boats, the woman probably only irritably urging him to hurry up so they can go home. Somewhere close by the sudden mocking laughter of seagulls. I smile at the little drama I have spun from nowhere, at its instant disintegration before my eyes.

I turn back to look at the sea, the great sweep of water stretching away to the far distant horizon and on to encircle the earth. I stand gazing upon it for some time, the soft wind on my face, my breath falling in time with its ebb and flow. And as I stand there, a panoramic vision of the past year opens up before me, as if with a cartographer's eye I finally survey its peaks and troughs laid out before me. I think of how completely our lives had been derailed. What had it been but a lusting, a raw hunger for continuation. For participation in the heart, the very marrow and essence of things.

My thoughts spin on, the daydream sprouting wings, becoming airborne. Rabbits bolting for cover. Little wagtails bursting indignantly upward from the scrubby undergrowth. I see Johnny stretched out on a lilo, the peaceful undulation of water passing through him as he bobs across the pool. Even from up here, I can see he is content. Close by him, Tamsin yawns from her sun bed, while the children play in the shade of a mimosa tree, though they are no more than specks now, like dancing insects. High on the eddies of wind, dipping down over the tree canopy, a fleeting glimpse of two spread-eagled teenagers making love amongst the pine trees, their scooter lying hastily discarded nearby. And passing onwards, over the top of an old finca, with washing hung out to dry, there – far, far below – was Arnie, tending his marijuana plants that grew so high he was almost lost from view as he walked amongst them. And it comes to me that we are all moving in time with the same ebb and flow. All responding to the same felt melody.

And out on a circuit across the bay, the pulsing waves beating perfect time too, and up, up, up again, the air perceptibly chilling, through fine wisps of clouds that throw off the unmistakable smell of ice crystals. Then the dazzling hot shout of sun, and banking back towards the coast, borne with a lovely ease, to find a woman, who can only be myself, standing perfectly still, cupped by the curve of the bay, entirely one with the great sweep of land and sea.

I come to, momentarily stumbling, and take up a pebble, smooth and round like a cool pigeon's egg, and put it carefully in my pocket. Then turn to retrace my footsteps up the long winding road. After a while I hear the hum of the fisherman's car climbing behind me. I glance quickly as it draws level. The man and woman silhouetted, apparently laughing now, she reaches over to kiss him, and then they are gone.

At the bottom of my sponge bag that night, I find an empty bottle of Buserelin, and throw it away with a buoyant sensation of closing a chapter – of at last walking forward.

The children sit in the back amongst the snaggle of ropes and broken farm equipment, while the engine hammers and leaps beneath us, labouring noisily up the steep mountain road. Arnie beats the steering wheel in time to a Doors' tape that blasts from the cassette machine, and revs the engine on. We had bumped into him again as we were buying provisions in the local town. The Bhagwan Rajneesh had once had a commune there and the notice boards were still cluttered with information on yoga classes and spiritual workshops drawn in an exotic mix and match profusion from Africa and the far East. Even the little supermarket kept a lunar calendar in the window. Arnie had greeted us like old friends, and invited us to a beach party. 'It's full moon tonight. Everyone goes crazy.'

I'd agreed unhesitatingly, but afterwards, Johnny had been angry with me. 'The man's a fraud, Rose. He's just some seedy old drug dealer, posing as a New Age visionary.' But eventually he'd succumbed to the children's pleas that we should go. Tamsin had waved us off, the baby at her hip, Pete beside her. 'Be good, kids,' he'd shouted after the departing truck. 'And if you can't be good, be careful . . .'

At each corner a half-empty bottle of tequila clatters from under the seat and strikes my ankles. But I can't lean down to retrieve it, the three of us packed so tightly together on the fraying seat, and Johnny cradling Arnie's African drum on his lap. A picture of Ganesh dangles from the rear-view mirror, gaily spinning and twisting at each sharp bend. As we reach the top of the mountain and begin the descent down the other side, the children shout in delight, pointing wildly. Below us, where the side of the road falls steeply away, two rusting cars lay belly up, half buried in undergrowth.

'Came off the road in the rainy season,' Arnie shouts over one shoulder. As the road levels out, we spin on through a little town, whitewashed buildings draped gaily in fiesta bunting, pausing only for an elderly peasant woman in traditional dress, who crosses the road at a stately pace.

'Can you believe she left me,' Arnie shouts, picking

up speed again through the water mirages that lie across the long stretch of road beyond. The earth is a ruddy colour here, even the sheep stained a russet red.

'Who?'

'Ursula. That girl who was waiting for me in the truck that time. When I woke up this morning, she was gone. All her clothes. Most of her paintings. She said she needed space to unblock her chakras.' He glances quickly at us and shrugs. *That's life, what can you do?* the shrug implies, though his face is stricken for a moment. Then he reaches abruptly for the volume knob and turns the music up. One of the dogs begins to howl an accompaniment, and from the back comes the children's shrieks of laughter again.

We sweep down the long track to the beach, cars parked helter-skelter for a mile back, and park where we can. The heat of the day is only just easing as I lift the children down onto the road. They skip about us, elated by the festivity in the air. People are streaming past us in groups of twos and threes, some carrying drums. Most are barefooted, women wearing jewellery that clinks and jingles at each step, and tattooed men, some with shaven heads or dreadlocks and piercings that catch the half-light.

The revellers cross the beach, backlit by the late afternoon sun, sand rising in gentle drifts at their feet. We stop to buy ice creams for the children before joining the swelling crowds at the far end of the bay. 'Let me know if you spot her, won't you?' Arnie walks with the drum clasped tightly, anxiously scanning the press of suntanned faces all about us. The babble of European tongues swells in volume, half-naked children scrambling through the sprawling adults who loll cross-legged everywhere, passing chillums that fill the evening air with a scent like sweet cedarwood. We find a space and sit down amongst them. Lily's ice cream runs across her chin, falling in gloopy drips between her fingers onto the flanks of her bare legs, as she eats in a rapt reverie of pleasure. I think for a moment that I might have glimpsed Ursula, but the woman is quickly lost from view again. It's only then I realise we have lost Arnie somewhere amongst the jostling crowds.

At the centre of the throng, enthroned on the terrace of a derelict fisherman's hut, twenty or thirty drummers sit motionless, looking out to sea, watching and waiting as the sun slips lower. They are an eclectic group; amongst them a beautiful ink-black man, naked but for a turban, a grey-haired woman who might be a university academic, a long-haired biker dressed like a Viking in loincloth and biker boots. One man looks like a weightlifter, his head shaved except for a long plait that snakes down his back. Beside him a woman with a radiant face, dressed in Indian clothes, suckling a child at her breast.

Then, at some unseen signal, as the sun begins its final descent towards the horizon, the drummers at last take up their drums and begin their rhythm. Tamsin's children rise up, beating time too as the pounding pulses through the very ground beneath us. Next to us, a pixie-faced hippy girl hands her baby to a friend and shyly takes up her drum. I catch a sudden glimpse of Arnie furiously drumming amongst the crowds, the sinews on his arms writhing like snakes, his hands a blur of motion, then he is lost from view again. Close by, a man with a crazy smile whirls like a dervish while from the far side of the crowd a brown-limbed girl in a crocheted bikini begins a mirror dance towards him. She shimmies through the revellers that divide them, until finally united they spin together.

'Christ, Rose. What have you got me into *now*?' Johnny's voice close against my ear, just discernible through the thunder. 'Bloody Arnie.' We turn to one another laughing at how absurdly incongruous we seem amongst this orgiastic pagan festival, yet disarmed despite ourselves by its sheer exuberance. As the sun sinks lower, touches the horizon, then slides at last from view, one of the drummers lifts a conch to his lips and at its melancholy bark, the thundering instantly ceases. I lean close. At last I can say it.

'It's you I want, Johnny. Nothing else matters.'

'Full moon's obviously gone to your head,' he says, straining for lightness, before drawing me close with a grave expression, and encircling me tightly with his arms.

All about us candles glimmer in the twilight that is now falling across the beach, their flames dipping and rising as a westerly breeze blows in from the ocean. A little way down the beach, a crowd is gathering around fire-eaters, their exhalations flaring like dragon's breath into the night sky. And already a great bloated moon is gliding up from behind the silhouetted pine trees.

* * *

I let myself drift this way and that across the silvery surface of the pool, a soothing sensation of cool water pleasantly buffering the scorch of hot air just beyond. I am weightless, an insubstantial thing. No more than an inhalation of breath. Now an exhalation.

Through the mass of water comes an almost imperceptible vibrato, steadily growing in intensity. If we weren't so far from civilisation I would think it sounded exactly like the grumbling bass of an approaching car. Then the pebbly crunch of something coming to a rest close by, followed by the heavy clunk of doors. I raise my head quickly, shaking water from my ears.

Someone who bears a startling resemblance to Bo Fisher stands straightening her dress beside a red hire car. And behind her, someone who appears to bear an even more startling resemblance to Bill Kelly, stretches then yawns. He leans into the car, and begins unbuckling the belt of a small boy who raises his arms to be released. I watch in disbelief, the noise of cicadas like the unoiled screech of a spinning wheel. As Bill lifts his son out of the car and turns towards us, it is as if he has stepped in three dimension from the inky square of that once coveted photograph. And behind them Arnie too now emerges from the car, pausing only to tweak the boy's cheek before waving a jaunty farewell to us all, and heading off down the track.

A pulse beats fast and loud at my temples, shock flooding my very being, a fever surely the most plausible explanation for this terrible hallucination. Or was it the onset of sunstroke? Or quite possibly madness? I blink and blink again as Bill and Bo approach the house, smiling odd smirks of triumph, a bottle of wine dangling casually from one hand. Behind them comes Noah, trotting to keep up.

'Well, what do you know . . .' Johnny raises his eyebrows sardonically at me. 'Mr Postcard from Paradise finally shows up,' he says before falling face down into the pool with a crash.

Tamsin hurries from the house frowning, then her mouth falls open. 'I don't believe it! How on earth did you find us?' She throws her arms out to greet them.

'Jesus!' Bill says. 'Talk about the back of beyond.'

'Rose . . .' Tamsin turns towards me. 'Do you . . . I can't remember if you've met . . . Rose, Johnny – this is Bill and Bo. Who are on their way – it's all coming back to me now – to a wedding in . . . Formentera?'

I wait to see what Bill will say, but he merely nods a greeting, holding my eye for a little longer than is comfortable, perhaps a hint of irony sharpening his smile. Beside him, Bo nods too, seeming not to recall me from our brief photo session together.

'You're never going to believe this.' Bo addresses us all. 'Ever since we landed, Bill's had this bee in his bonnet about dropping by on a surprise visit. So we set off, right. Can't get a peep out of the mobile. Get *completely* lost. Of course. No map and not a soul in sight. Typical us. And Bill's in a right old strop. 'Cause it's all *my* fault. As usual. And I'm like, "That's it. We're going home!" So we turn the car round, nearly run down that old hippy out walking his dogs. And there's me – in my best Spanish,

"*Pardone signor. Donde est* the castle?" And he's like,
"Young lady. I will take you there myself!" '

'Well hallelujah for Arnie!' Tamsin shakes her head
wonderingly, and leans down to the little boy. 'Hello
Noah, my precious. Aren't we lucky.'

With one wet finger in his mouth, the child grimaces
sullenly up at her, holding his father's hand tightly.
Though he has grown since the photograph, I recognise
him only too well. Bill strolls with him to the edge of the
pool, looking down on us like a creature from another
world.

'So here you are!' Tamsin begins dragging sun-
loungers forward for them, plumping up cushions.

'Here we are!' Bill agrees, smiling down at Johnny and
me, as he dangles Noah playfully over the water.

While lunch preparations overtake the day, I seek quiet
anonymity in the shadows, afraid my trembling hands
will betray me. Once the meal is served, in a panic that
we must all sit for a while in enforced proximity, I take
up my discarded camera from the bottom of the suitcase.
To retreat behind it seems, for the moment anyway, the
best I can hope for.

I train the lens on Pete as he regales everyone with a
recent saga. I capture a moment or two of his animation,
his hands outstretched in mock exasperation, and a
kind of calm begins to fall, the trembling easing away.
With the familiar weight of the camera in my hands and
its buffer at my eye, I have disappeared. I focus now
on Tamsin. In the bright square of my viewfinder,

she listens to the conversation, smiling reflectively. After a moment, she drops a gentle cheek to rest on Lily's drowsy head. But hearing the clunk of the aperture she turns.

'Oh, hello there,' she says, smiling a self-conscious camera smile. 'The photographer's back then.' And looking up, Lily flaps a hand at me, twisting away, butting her mother's shoulder and whining. So I pan on, and settle instead on Johnny, who is laughingly interjecting in Pete's story. With the aperture wide open, the sea and trees beyond him are no more than drifts of abstract colour. In this world, it's as if intruders have never burst so alarmingly upon us.

At the meal's end I rise hastily, muttering something about a siesta, and withdraw to my room. With any luck they would be on their way while I slept. But when I re-emerge later that afternoon I find that a reordering of the sleeping arrangements has been made and Bill and Bo have agreed to stay the night. The two of them are lolling together in the hammock, Bo lying with a blissful expression, while Bill rubs suntan oil into her back. The strangest sensation, a covetous laceration, before I turn quickly away again.

As the fierce afternoon heat begins at last to ease, I can't seem to shake the acute and painful awareness of him. Though I'm careful to keep my distance, his presence and even his very absence press upon me. Once, passing by the pool, I glance down to find him sliding past underwater, only inches from my bare feet, and the gleaming brown back scorches my eyes again, jolting the tremor back into my hands. More than once I sense his amused eyes upon me, and the disconcerting realisation comes to me, that it is I now who am spied upon. *Why had he come? What did he want from me?*

When evening falls, I decline the invitation to join everyone for dinner at a nearby restaurant. Though Johnny tries vainly to persuade me, I am sullenly resolute in my refusal. As the sound of their car disappears away down the track, I walk the house, the quarry tiles cool underfoot, my jangled nerves calming now his watchful eye is no longer upon me. By tomorrow they would be gone, and we could resume our lives.

I sit on the terrace for a while. Far away the farmer's donkey was braying. I listen, my breath slipping from me. A lilac cast has fallen upon the sky and land, a velvet stain like a bruise along the horizon. It was still tonight. No whisper of breeze from the sea.

The memory of Bill oiling Bo's back, leaning over her with a slow hand, fleets through me. And instantly the restless trepidation comes again, a flutter of anticipatory dread. The agitation in my limbs forces me up from my seat. Small creatures in the wild became restless in just this way, I think. Sniffing the air in alarm as the predator drew nearer, but somehow held fast, running in ever diminishing circles. When Johnny returns at midnight, mutual remorse makes our lovemaking a tender reunion.

That night the moon shines so brilliantly through our window, its strange milky fluorescence bathes the bed, making it appear we are on board a boat adrift in darkness. I lie in the heat of the night, twisting first one way, then the other. And when sleep finally comes, my dreams are feverish and troubled.

From sky to sea is a continuous sweep this morning, a watercolour blur merging them as one. Little triangular boats cross to and fro as if sailing dreamily through sky. I sit in a daze, the stupor of the night still upon me. Then the children burst abruptly from the house. 'A boat ride, a boat ride! We're all going on a boat ride!' they shriek, the slap of their excited feet stampeding past.

'Boat ride?' Johnny looks up from his book. A surprise expedition, Pete explains, appearing behind them, setting down a pile of clean beach towels amongst the breakfast things. He has hired a fisherman's boat, he says, and plans to take us all for a picnic to a nearby beach that can only be reached by sea.

Johnny nods enthusiastically. 'Oh great. A test run for our round-the-world trip. Good thinking, Captain.' Further enthusiasm greets the plan when Bill and Bo sleepily emerge, both readily agreeing to delay their departure to the evening.

'Hey, guys!' Bo claps her hands at the children. 'We get to go on a cruise!'

I can see a tiny reflection of myself in Pete's sunglasses. I open my mouth to make my excuses. Then close it again. Can't face the protests if I resist joining them again. And anyway, I think angrily, this man is nothing to me – why should I fear him?

Lying quietly on the lilo, I drift on the cross-currents of water hoping to conjure invisibility again. An exasperated Pete is trying to get everyone organised, calling irritable instructions. He moves between the house and car, staggering under the weight of sun tents and buckets, struggling to find space for everything in the boot. The children are squabbling, and Tamsin's scolding voice floats from the kitchen.

Too late, far far too late, the sight of Bill standing at the poolside jolts me from my trance. A flash of blurred movement through air. The shocking crash of breaking water. An eerie silence as his fractured form snakes beneath the water, before bursting beside me, silvery rivulets streaming from him. Heart leap-frogging. At the fingers gripping the lilo, at the gleam of teeth and eye so shockingly close now. And yet the oddest impulse to reach out, to trace the wet curve of shoulder.

'Fate brings us together again then,' he says with a disarming smile. In the far distance beyond him, Pete still moves to and fro.

'So it seems . . .'

'What on earth became of you that night? Where the hell did you go?'

'I . . . I meant to call you . . .'

He regards me closely, seeming not only to sense my trepidation, but to be excited, goaded even by it.

'It was like I'd dreamt you. One minute, there we were

talking. Next you'd vanished into the night like some will-o'-the-wisp . . .'

'I wasn't well. I'm sorry. It was unforgivable . . .' Never have such avid eyes been fixed upon me.

'Wasn't something I did then?'

We gaze at each other, half-blinded by the blaze of light that flares across the pool, and I shake my head. The fleetingly lovely scent of suntan oil. A peppery flare of wild rosemary. Then a crash of water again, and Johnny is surfacing beside us.

'Bliss!' He drifts onto his back, spitting a celebratory plume of water into the air.

'Christ! Are you coming or what?' Pete stands at the edge, hands on hips, surveying the three of us. 'Let's get a bloody move on, shall we?'

'Yes, Dad . . .' Johnny hauls himself out again. 'Coming, Dad.'

I catch the quick flash of a wolfish smile, before Bill dips wordlessly beneath the surface, and I am spun free, pitching and rolling on the choppy waters.

We lie with the debris of the picnic all about us, the afternoon's sun a fierce roar now. Tamsin is fretting about keeping the baby shaded, but the sun tent keeps collapsing and we have all drunk a little too much to address its repair practically. I leave them struggling and wade into the water with a snorkel and flippers, aware only of the press of heat. All coherent thought long gone, not even the unease of those hawk-like eyes upon me as I strike out across the bay, heading for the rock that rises steeply from the sea.

Down here in this underworld, time is entirely suspended. Fish darting away through spangled bracelets of light, disappearing with a flash of tail into the felty pelt of seaweed. I chug slowly, caressed by sudden blood warm pockets of water, until at length, feeling the deep throb of the motorboat low in the water, I turn back to the shore, kicking my way like a stately paddle steamer, enjoying the little shoals darting in a v-formation before me.

But rising up from the sea, shaking water from my hair, I'm puzzled to find Bill lying alone on the beach now. I step back, but the vigorous surf pushes me forward. Again my feet scrabble for resistance in the sucking undertow, but forwards the surf boils again, toppling me on my way. I scan the beach wildly, praying for familiar figures to gambol merrily into view. How could they all simply have vanished? Then one last vigorous wave spits me forth, thrusting me on unsteady feet towards him.

He leans up on one elbow, watching my approach. Only the sea's hot breath at my back.

'Where's everyone gone?' The panic in my voice undisguised.

He flops back lazily. 'Kids were getting crabby. Tamsin and Bo decided they needed a kip. Johnny's gone along to help out. But Pete promised he'd be back for us as quickly as he could . . .'

Thoughts skidding and crashing in alarm. The journey there and back could easily take an hour. I sit down on the towel, pulling it as far away as politeness allows. Stretch out cautiously, time moving in slow motion, the skin on my arms blanching at his proximity, at the unbearable exposure.

'I mean, I don't know about you, but I'm far too fucked to be going anywhere,' he mutters drowsily.

Christ, oh Christ, oh Christ. Thrumming over and over in my head, colliding with itself. *Christ, oh Christ, oh Christ. Feign sleep*, my jangled brain instructs. *Just lie quietly till Pete returns*.

Yawning conspicuously, I settle carefully on the island of the towel. Within its boundaries all will be well. When Pete arrives, I can simply startle into life again like Snow White. I stretch out, wishing the hammering at my throat would cease and close my eyes. One last stagey yawn.

Let calm come.

Sea water streaming from me, running in warm tributaries along the insides of my legs. Pray that the fiery air might become a shield. Only the thud of blood, the pulse of sea now.

'Such a shame to leave unfinished business between us, Rosie Posie . . .'

A sudden rustle of whirring wings, or possibly the hiss of a serpent, and the red glow behind my eyelids darkens as something, or someone, blocks out the sun. The warmth of his face upon mine. The shock of his hand soft across my belly. Desire like a bee sting of adrenalin through every synapse of my body, quite instantaneous.

14

The swelling stomach is a new journey. Friends congratulate us warmly, genuine emotion resonating in their voices. 'Isn't it extraordinary,' they say, 'how often it's only when you've accepted it's not to be, and just relax, that it finally happens.' And we agree, Johnny and I, shaking our heads and smiling too at the magnificent mystery of it all. Sometimes, he places a hand on the swollen globe of my belly, and laughs in sheer delighted astonishment, recalling the fateful night when the moon had shone so brightly through our bedroom window. We call it the miracle of Tanit, and joke that the island could become a place of pilgrimage for infertile couples.

All those bleak cycles, that long suspension. It's as if I have thrown aside the blinkers of self-absorption to find Johnny still walking loyally in step beside me. In what feels a ceremonial moment, we throw open the spare room, at last naming it as the nursery, and fill it with all the paraphernalia that a small baby will apparently require. Johnny's father has carved a wooden rocking horse, my parents donate the family cot and Tamsin shyly shows me the bags of carefully folded baby clothes she has been saving for me all this time. 'We are blessed, truly blessed,' Johnny often says, the light of gratitude so bright in his eyes, I can't help the tiny shard of glass that twists so sharply in my heart. And that is all that lies between true redemption and me. Knowing and not knowing.

The labour is long and fierce, Johnny beside me, an anxious traveller in the storm. And the baby when he finally comes is a downy sea-fruit, tumbling lithe and ripe into my arms, howling a lusty ululation of new life. Johnny takes him with infinite care, holding him close, stroking the top of his head over and over with his lips.

'Hello there, little fellow. Hello. You've been one hell of a long time coming,' he croons, traces of blood streaking his cheek. 'What kept you?'

You are our end and our beginning, I think, blinded by tears. Our beginning and our end.

Acknowledgements

My thanks to:

Sammy Lee, to whom I shall always be deeply indebted.
To many old friends, amongst them: Paul Greengrass for invaluable feedback at the beginning, and Annabel Hackney, Matt Byam Shaw, Denise Dorrance, Paul Yule, Dominic Turner and Olly Lambert for their input along the way. My editors, Suzanne Baboneau and Rochelle Venables for unstinting tact and rigour throughout.
And of course my husband, Andy Harries, without whom none of this would have been possible.

I am also indebted to the following authors and books:

Counselling in Male Infertility – Sammy Lee (Blackwell Science);
Male Infertility: Men Talking – Mary-Claire Mason (Sheldon Press);
The IVF Revolution – *Professor Robert Winston* (Vermillion).